# HE'D BEEN DRINKING...
*and there was lipstick at the corner of his mouth.*

She glared at him. "May I go now, Dr. Raymond?" she asked coldly.

He was crumpling the letter of introduction, and she watched him drop it carelessly into the waste basket before he looked at her again.

"I'll see you at dinner," he said. "There's one thing though. You've come to the right place to forget. All tensions fade away on the good ship *Nirvana*. It's the same every cruise, with everyone finding a beatific oblivion to care, pain, memories, failures, and reality. They call it having fun, and it's the in-thing on the *S. S. Nirvana*...."

He was lighting a cigarette as she closed the door, and back in her own cabin she sat on the bunk and discovered that she was trembling, and close to tears.

# SIGNET Nurse-Doctor Titles You Will Enjoy

☐ **NURSE LAMBERT'S CONFLICT by Diana Douglas.** A beautiful, dedicated nurse is besought with conflict when her love life interferes with her career. (#P4099—60¢)

☐ **BACKSTAGE NURSE by Jane Converse.** A fading child star finds life intolerable until Nurse Banks enters the picture. (#P4069—60¢)

☐ **SKI LODGE NURSE by Diana Douglas.** A lovely young nurse at a ski resort finds herself surrounded by terror and danger. (#T4161—75¢)

☐ **ICE SHOW NURSE by Jane Converse.** The beautiful young nurse followed the doctor to the ice show to be near him, but he had eyes only for the temperamental star. (#P4121—60¢)

☐ **JET SET NURSE by Jane Converse.** A beautiful young nurse accompanies a jet set party on a Caribbean cruise. Her job is to take charge of the beautiful but "sick" daughter of the hostess, a young girl who is a threat to herself and everyone else on the trip. (#P4221—60¢)

---

**THE NEW AMERICAN LIBRARY, INC., P.O. Box 2310, Grand Central Station, New York, New York 10017**

Please send me the SIGNET BOOKS I have checked above. I am enclosing $_____(check or money order—no currency or C.O.D.'s). Please include the list price plus 10¢ a copy to cover mailing costs. (New York City residents add 6% Sales Tax. Other New York State residents add 3% plus any local sales or use taxes.)

Name_____

Address_____

City_____State_____Zip Code_____

Allow at least 3 weeks for delivery

# *SEA NURSE*

## DIANA DOUGLAS

A SIGNET BOOK from
**NEW AMERICAN LIBRARY**
TIMES MIRROR
in association with Horwitz Publications

© Copyright 1970 by Horwitz Publications, Sydney, Australia

Reproduction in part or in whole in any language expressly forbidden in any part of the world without the written consent of Horwitz Publications.

All rights reserved

SIGNET TRADEMARK REG. U.S. PAT. OFF. AND FOREIGN COUNTRIES
REGISTERED TRADEMARK—MARCA REGISTRADA
HECHO EN CHICAGO, U.S.A.

SIGNET, SIGNET CLASSICS, MENTOR AND PLUME BOOKS
are published by The New American Library, Inc.,
1301 Avenue of the Americas, New York, New York 10019

FIRST PRINTING, JUNE, 1970

PRINTED IN THE UNITED STATES OF AMERICA

# CHAPTER ONE

The office of the South Seas Shipping Company towered high above the bay, five blocks up the hill from the San Francisco waterfront.

The neat gold lettering on the office door read *Reginald Plymouth—Director*. A rather burly, gray-haired man in his fifties, he appeared engrossed in the small file of papers he was studying, but in fact he was shrewdly evaluating the girl sitting on the other side of the huge desk.

Her appointment had already been decided by the personnel manager, Talbot Reese, although the girl waiting patiently was unaware of this. It now only remained for him to give his approval to Reese's decision to employ her as senior nurse for the cruise ship *Nirvana*.

The girl's appearance was certainly consistent with what the shipping line sought in female staff ashore or at sea. She was tall, slim, and attractive; her clothes were smart but conservative. A blonde with large, intelligent gray eyes, she seemed neither impatient nor nervous as he kept her waiting. She had an air of calm about her that he liked.

And the recommendations he had just finished skimming through were on a par with her appearance. At any other time he would have slashed his signature across the appointment beneath Reese's at once, but it was a remark of Reese's that made him hesitate.

Reese had said, "This one isn't the usual type, sir. She could be the best nurse we've employed in years. If we can keep her. . . ."

Plymouth looked up at her now and smiled reassuringly. "You have very good testimonials, Miss Madison. I understand that Mr. Reese explained to you the nature of your duties on the S.S. *Nirvana*. You know therefore that the passengers are not the usual run of tourists one expects to find on a cruise ship. The *Nirvana* is in fact known in shipping circles as a millionaire cruise ship. Many of our passengers are elderly, and confidentially, rather spoiled people. They could prove difficult patients for a nurse whose experience has been confined to hospital work, no matter how efficient she may be. Have you thought about that, Miss Madison?"

She smiled fleetingly, an attractive smile, but one that faded quickly.

"I have," she admitted. "But I feel confident I can manage. Being difficult when sick isn't the prerogative of any particular class. Sometimes it's a reaction to sickness, or surroundings, or simply being managed. You learn to accept this, and treat them tactfully. If you can't, you shouldn't be a nurse."

He nodded approval. What she had said, he decided, was neither too little nor too much.

"I believe you'll manage very well, Miss Madison," he said quietly. He glanced down at the file again. "I notice that you were recently appointed charge nurse in the postoperative ward at the Medical Center, and that you showed considerable organizational ability. From our viewpoint this is excellent. However, it also brings a question to mind. Why give up such a promising career in hospital nursing to become a nurse on a cruise ship? The immediate salary we offer may be higher, but the possibilities for further advancement are just not there. What you become when you step onto the deck of the *Nirvana* is what you can expect to be ten years from now, if you stay with us. I find myself wondering why you have made this choice."

For the first time he saw uncertainty come into those clear gray eyes, and she hesitated before she said slowly, "I needed a change, Mr. Plymouth. For . . . personal reasons." Her eyes looked past him, seeing something beyond the windows.

"If I'm curious," he persisted gently, "it's because you're not like most of the girls I interview from time to time. Usually they're attractive, and plausible. They have all the answers certainly, but leave me with the impression that they're more concerned with the prospect of a glamour cruise than nursing."

"Yet you accept them?"

She was shrewd too, he decided. He smiled. "If their recommendations suggest they are also efficient nurses, yes, we do, Miss Madison. But of course we have our own methods of checking them out thoroughly before we sign them on."

As you probably have done with me, Lindy Madison thought. She frowned. What did it matter? The personnel manager had probably talked to someone at the Medical Center to find out the reason. And someone there had probably told him. It seemed strange suddenly that she should feel so reluctant to tell him, that she felt the need to hide what had happened. That she didn't want to speak of things that had hurt her so deeply. . . .

But the feeling was strong, and she had to fight it.

That was why she merely said, "A cruise ship has always seemed to me like a small, self-contained city. The people on it, crew as well as passengers, have accidents and become sick the same as other people. Therefore they need skilled help and hospitalization. I don't expect to lose what nursing skill I have for want of practice. It isn't the glamour of cruising that interests me, believe it or not, Mr. Plymouth. I applied for the position because it seemed so different from anything I've done before. I hoped to be so busy that I wouldn't have time to think . . . about myself." Her gray eyes studied his face. "Haven't you ever felt like that? That you just *had* to . . . to get away from everything you've ever known?"

He nodded, frowning suddenly. "Most people have, Miss Madison. I felt like that three years ago. I lost someone very dear to me."

Unexpectedly then, he saw pity come into her eyes. And something else. She was going to tell him now, he knew instinctively.

"I'm sorry," she murmured. "I shouldn't have asked you that. . . ."

"No," he said. "It's better not to keep such things locked away. This happens, and you learn to live with it. I lost my wife from terminal cancer, Miss Madison. She had both strength and courage, so it was very slow and painful for all concerned. I traveled for a year, but it's better to work, so I came back here. I'm glad now that I did."

She nodded. "Something like that happened to me," she said in a low voice. "My fiancé died at the Medical Center in Los Angeles. He had leukemia. I wasn't permitted to nurse him, of course, but I saw him every day. I could see . . . everything that was happening to him. I . . ." She broke off, and he saw there were tears in her eyes and was sorry he'd pushed it so far. "Nursing is my life," she added slowly. "It has been since I entered nursing school. I'll go back to hospital nursing in a year or two perhaps. I suppose I'm . . . running away. But there are too many memories back there."

He nodded and stood up. "Come over to the window, Miss Madison."

She stood up and followed him. The office windows looked across the Embarcadero and the waterfront. On the Sausalito shore two yachts sailing toward the Golden Gate were heeling far over in the stiff breeze.

"There's the *Nirvana*," he said, pointing down. "Lying at Pier Eleven."

The white ship rested against the pier, her decks busy with the crew loading stores and luggage.

"Yes. The *Nirvana* is a fine ship. In ten days' time the passengers will begin to go aboard. Wealth doesn't always bring happiness, so there will be some among them trying to forget troubles as bitter as yours, or mine. A few will find escape, find the peace of mind they seek. I hope that happens to you too, Miss Madison, and I believe it will. We'd like you to go aboard as soon as possible. Mr. Reese will give you a letter of introduction to the ship's surgeon, sign you on, and arrange for your inoculations."

She murmured her thanks and shook the firm hand he offered her. He laughed, deliberately breaking the tension, and patted her shoulder as he walked her to the door.

"Good luck and a pleasant voyage, Miss Madison," he said cheerfully. "You're young and the company doesn't expect you to work *all* the time. I hope you stay with us, and remember there are other avenues in this organization that do offer opportunities for high advancement, even if nursing does not. You seem to me to have character and dedication, and these are traits we value here."

Walking back to his desk he thought unexpectedly, "How I would have liked her to nurse Leah. . . ."

The days before the sailing of the S.S. *Nirvana* passed quickly for Melinda Madison. The inoculations brought an unexpected reaction of fever, headache, and a sore arm that prevented her from going aboard immediately.

When the fever passed and she reported to Talbot Reese, she found that her cabin and the sick bay on the *Nirvana* were being painted and refitted for the cruise. He sent her for her second round of inoculations and told her to take the week off. She was glad for this, as San Francisco was unexplored territory to her. She spent the time window-shopping and exploring the city. She liked its gardens, hills, and quaint cable cars, and the green and brown ranges beyond the blue water of the Bay. And she was fascinated by Chinatown.

If she stayed with the shipping line this would be her home port, and she found herself liking that idea more and more as sailing day approached.

And on the cruise she would see foreign places even more interesting, even if they failed to create the same affection. Honolulu, Fiji, Tahiti, Auckland, Sydney, Melbourne. . . .

She began to grow impatient to go aboard and was glad when Reese ordered her to report to his office with her luggage twenty-four hours before sailing time.

Leaving the personnel office she glanced at the letter Talbot Reese had given her introducing her to the ship's surgeon, Dr. Raymond. Reese had assured her she would find him an excellent surgeon and an easy man to work with.

*Dr. Raymond, ship's surgeon, S.S. Nirvana, Pier Eleven.*

Lindy Madison frowned, studying the name typed on the front of the envelope. Raymond? Raymond. . . ? She remembered suddenly, and her frown became a bright smile. Of course! *Peter* Raymond! How could she have forgotten? She'd had quite a crush on Peter Raymond when he was resident surgeon at the Los Angeles Medical Center. But that had been two years ago, and so much had happened since.

Roy Bryant, fascinating, lovable Roy, had intervened. She had fallen in love with him, and then the disease had set in. It had been as though her own life had ended with Roy's death.

She sighed and put the letter back in her

handbag, wondering if the doctor on the *Nirvana* could possibly be the Peter Raymond she had known. Peter had been well-known at the Center as a serious and dedicated young surgeon. Not at all the type she would expect to work on a glamorous cruise ship.

He had gone East when his residency ended, and the last she had heard he had been assisting a big-name heart surgeon in New York. That was over a year ago. Before she met Roy.

But she smiled, remembering Peter Raymond as she went down to her waiting taxi.

"Pier Eleven, please. S.S. *Nirvana*."

She remembered that Peter had often been the main topic of conversation among the nurses. But he'd always kept very much to himself.

On the rare occasions when he did seek a partner for some social function, he never asked the same girl out twice. Lindy had admired him for that, understanding his reasoning. He had dedicated himself to his profession, and the achievement of a high degree of surgical skill was a full-time job.

Yet she had been as attracted by his good looks as all the other girls. When he had asked her to be his partner at a New Year's Eve party at the home of a house surgeon, she had been delighted. It was the talk of the nursing staff. It had been a wonderful night, too, she recalled nostalgically. They had danced and laughed all night. She could remember her hand in his and the gentle, affectionate kiss when they'd parted in the dawn outside the nurses' home.

But soon she had met Roy, and shortly afterward Peter Raymond had completed the years of his residency at the Medical Center and left for New York. She remembered that she had meant to say good-bye, but Roy had been ill. . . .

With the passing months, Roy had always seemed ill, she remembered sadly. The family doctor had treated him for anemia, but nobody suspected his increasing illness and debility were the insidious advance of leukemia. Not that it would have made much difference, she admitted. It had already been too late. . . .

Melinda Madison sighed as the taxi pulled up to the curb. Her attention turned to the graceful white bulk of the *Nirvana* thrusting high above the wharf.

She felt a shiver of excitement when she saw the ship at close quarters. From the dockside it looked huge. The officer at the top of the companionway directed her to the purser's office, where she picked up her keys. The purser had a curly brown beard, mutton-chop side whiskers, and twinkling brown eyes that examined her with admiration as he welcomed her aboard.

"You're to report to Dr. Raymond," he smiled. "But right now he isn't on board. He went ashore about an hour ago with Miss Kent, our other nurse. I'll tell him you're here when he gets back. If he runs true to form that should be about five bells in the second dog watch. Then you'll see the sick-bay door open. Just go in."

She stared at him blankly for a moment before she noticed his sly smile. Wary of the expression on his face, she decided not to ask him what a "dog watch" was and merely thanked him.

As she was leaving, the steward said, "If there's anything you want to know about the ship at any time, Miss Madison, come and see me. Okay?"

"Okay," she said doubtfully.

The purser watched her slim figure disappear down the passage. He knew that if he'd been Raymond, he would've waited to see what the new nurse was like before taking the other one out on the town.

The steward put down her bags at the staircase and flashed her a friendly grin. He was a small, blue-eyed, alert man, just beginning to gray at the temples.

"Have you ever been a ship's nurse before, Miss?"

"No, I've always worked in hospitals."

He nodded. "That's what I thought. Anyway, five bells in the second dog watch is six thirty this evening. And if you take a look around the corner here, you'll see the sick bay." He walked with her to the corner, steering her arm lightly. "There you are, Miss," he said, smiling. "You go in through Dr. Raymond's office. Dispensary and a small operating room with an annex, and I guess that's about it. The key to it will be with the others you have if you want to take a look after you've unpacked."

She flashed him a grateful smile. "Thank you. But I think I should wait until Dr. Raymond gets back."

"Sure." He studied her face briefly. "By the way, I'm Charley Kinsela. Your cabin is in my section. Miss Carter is your cabin stewardess, and any time you want her, just ring. She'll give you a timetable for meals, and tell you anything you want to know. If she can't help—just send for me. I'll show you your cabin now. Okay?"

"Thank you, Charley."

"Any time," he said cheerfully. "Dr. Raymond has enlisted me as a sick-bay attendant once or twice. I was a medic in the army. Had to give anesthetics and transfusions then, and I haven't forgotten how it's done." His cheerful grin was contagious as he added, "In a way that makes me feel like one of the hospital team again, if you know what I mean."

"I do know what you mean, Charley. It can be a good feeling." She hesitated. "What . . . is Dr. Raymond like to work with?"

He closed the elevator doors and glanced at her. "Dr. Raymond is a fine surgeon, Miss. I'd say he's wasted here, but no doubt he has his own reasons for that. And I'm sure you'll find him easy to get along with when he's working."

He lapsed into a silence that lasted until he had unlocked her cabin door and put her bags inside. He smiled again then.

"You'll be unpacking for a while, I guess. I'll have Miss Carter bring you some coffee at three thirty. And you don't have to worry about the ship's bells. The purser was having a little joke. Just adjust your watch by the ship's clock each morning. The door there opens into a bathroom, and you share it with Miss Kent. If there's anything else you want to know, ring for Miss Carter or me."

She smiled. "Thanks, Charley. You've been most helpful."

"Carter will make up your bed each evening

while you're having dinner. By day it's a lounge. She tidies up each morning while you're at breakfast."

When he had gone she looked around her cabin. Accommodation in nurses' homes, she decided, was never like this! Desk, closets, lighting, upholstery—everything—was smart and modern. She bounced experimentally on the long sofa that Charley had told her was her bed. A small partition gave the impression of a second room, where there was another small but comfortable sofa, coffee table, bookcase, and deep chairs.

Lindy Madison hadn't known quite what to expect, but the reality exceeded anything she had dreamed. A peek into the bathroom disclosed the same elegance. It was a good beginning to a new life.

She began to unpack her clothes and hang them in the roomy closets. She was astonished when the doorbell rang and a smiling stewardess came in with coffee and cookies on a tray. It was already three thirty.

The purser had said Dr. Raymond would not be back till six thirty. She went down in the elevator to the main deck in case he had already returned, but the door of the sick bay was still closed. She felt a bit relieved and went timidly exploring the lounges and public rooms. She admired the Tahitian Club and the South Seas Lounge, flanked by Polynesian-style bars. She became lost in the maze of passages among the upper-deck cabins.

On the boat deck, stewards were polishing glasses behind the bar. The deck was roofed, but open facing the stern of the ship and the large tiled swimming pool. The pool was empty, and the tiles clean and shining in readiness for it to be filled at sea.

The ship's clock showed five thirty as she left the elevator. The door of the sick bay was still closed, so she continued her tour. On the main deck she found the passengers' dining room. She also discovered a well-equipped theater, a beauty salon, barber shop, and a compact shopping center displaying everything one might need on the voyage. And all duty free once the ship was at sea.

Lindy Madison glanced at her watch. It was six thirty already. The main-deck exploration had taken longer than she thought. She hurried back, recognizing the chief steward's office, and turned the corner to the hospital. The door was ajar, and she could hear the murmur of voices inside as she touched the doorbell.

There was silence for a few moments before a deep, masculine voice said, "Come in."

A tall man with thick black hair was standing near the reception desk of a rather small outer office. He looked up at her and said curtly, "Yes?"

The first thing Lindy noticed was the smear of lipstick at the corner of his mouth. Then she saw the deep blue eyes, contrasting startlingly with the raven hair and the sun-tanned skin of his handsome face. She was surprised that he looked older, but recognized him to be the Peter Raymond she had known. He studied her impatiently.

She said uncertainly, "Mr. Reese asked that I report to you, Dr. Raymond. . . ."

"You're the new nurse?" The dark blue eyes swept over her in a way she did not like. "Mr. Reese's taste seems to be improving," he murmured. "I suppose they gave you the usual letter briefing me on your nursing skill, and glowing recommendations from your previous employers? Only the best is good enough for the S.S. *Nirvana*—even if all you'll have to do is dispense medication for hangovers and seasickness."

Lindy felt herself flush angrily as he held out his hand and she gave him the letter. The stale liquor on his breath was unmistakable.

He was watching her over the letter, his expression cynical. "You want me to labor through Reese's flowery eulogy, which never varies much—or shall we take it as read and adjourn to get ready for dinner, Miss. . . ?"

"The name is Madison, Doctor," she said resentfully. "And I think you should read the letter."

"Oh, you do, do you, Miss Madison?" He frowned, suddenly aggressive. Lindy steeled herself to meet an angry outburst, but behind him a door opened and a girl in a beige miniskirted suit came out replacing a compact in her purse, and he turned to grin at her. "Beth, we've a new member of the staff and she wants me to read one of Reese's letters." He looked back at Lindy, the cynical smile returning. "Meet Beth Kent, Miss. . . ? What did you say your name was?"

"Madison. Hello Miss Kent."

"Hello." Brown eyes studied Lindy speculatively, and with faint antagonism. She was a small girl, with a voluptuous figure and a pretty face.

He bent his head over the letter, frowning. They were both as high as kites, Lindy decided dismally. It didn't seem a good start. But perhaps she should make allowances. After all, she didn't know a thing about shipboard life, and if they'd both been off duty since this morning. . . .

"You're from the Medical Center at Los Angeles?" His tone had changed. "I went there from my internship for a two-year surgical residency under Dr. Feldman. But that would be before your time."

"No, Dr. Raymond," she said quietly. "I was Dr. Reinhardt Schmidt's scrub nurse while you were a house surgeon at the Center. I was there when you left for New York to work with Dr. Grayson."

She was aware of Beth Kent's quick, suspicious stare as he put the letter down to study her face again.

"I seem to remember . . ." he muttered doubtfully.

"We both worked in the surgical service, Doctor," she said.

"That was a long while ago." He said it slowly, pensively.

"About two years, I think," she replied calmly.

He nodded suddenly. "Of course, *Lindy* Madison? I remember you now! Is Schmidt still there? I haven't seen anyone from the Center since I left."

"Dr. Schmidt is still there. And Dr. Feldman."

"Well, well!" he said. He looked at Beth Kent. "You needn't wait, Beth. I'll see you at dinner. You'd better show Miss Madison our table, and brief her on dining-room customs and other ship nonsense. Okay?"

Beth Kent pouted at him, but nodded. She gave Lindy a spiteful glance in passing, and said sweetly, "Wear your uniform, Miss Madison. I'll call for you at seven fifteen."

Lindy murmured her thanks and stood waiting, feeling rather like a high school girl called out before a teacher, while the man at the desk studied her face. She heard the door close behind her.

"This letter says you were in charge of the postoperative wards," he said gruffly when the door closed.

"Yes, Doctor."

"As I remember, that would've been the way you wanted it. You were a good nurse, and you knew what you wanted."

"It *was* what I wanted then," she said, avoiding those probing blue eyes while she tried to stay calm and not become angry again.

"So why are you here now?" he asked bluntly.

Lindy felt her face flush. "I could ask you the same question, Dr. Raymond," she retorted. "The last I heard you were going to Bellevue to work with Dr. Roach in open-heart surgery. I've explained my reasons to Mr. Plymouth and he has accepted them. You know I can handle the work here. Does anything else matter?"

He gave her a tight, unfriendly smile. "It matters to me, Miss Madison. Reese has appointed you senior nurse. And this isn't a hospital. If you try to run it like one of the wards at the Center, the other nurses aren't going to like that. You'll find life on the *Nirvana* is different. Maybe that's why we're here. But what about you, why are you here? Did Plymouth offer you some other promotion? Something better later?"

Lindy studied the smear of lipstick near his mouth. "I'm here to work, the way I always have. I'm not here to try to change anything, if that's what you're thinking. I hoped this would be different from hospital work. I wanted to get away from *that* for . . . personal reasons, Doctor."

He leaned back in his chair and grinned unexpectedly. "Are you trying to tell me you're here just for the glamour cruise? Well, now I've heard everything. This isn't your kind of territory, Lindy! Not unless you've changed a lot since I knew you."

"As *you* obviously have," she said bitterly.

His grin widened. "We're discussing you, not me. Well?"

She hesitated. "I was going to be married. He . . . died at the Center. I . . . had to get away from there. I had to do something different. This seemed the answer. . . ."

"Oh, it is," he said. "Believe me, it is. Did you know I was here?"

She looked at him indignantly. "How could I?"

He nodded, and his smile faded. "I see. What was it with the guy?"

"He had leukemia," she said reluctantly.

"Leukemia?" He stared at her, surprised. "Acute leukemia?" Momentarily she glimpsed the Peter Raymond she had once known as she saw pity come into his eyes and he murmured, "You poor kid. . . !"

"It was myelogenous," she said quietly.

He frowned at her. "Myelogenous leukemia? That's terminal, but it takes three to four years. Surely you must have noticed symptoms? You must have seen what had already happened before you . . . got close to him? He must've had the bug for a year or two earlier. Don't tell me you couldn't read the signs?"

"Yes, I knew," she said quietly.

"Yet you were going to marry him? For God's sake, why?"

"Why do girls fall in love? It just seemed to happen, that's all." She had said it defensively, she realized. This made her feel guilty, and anger came into her gray eyes.

He looked away. "Sometimes we mistake pity for love," he said. "Goddamn it! How can you tell the difference, anyway?"

"It wasn't pity."

"Okay—it wasn't pity. You fell in love with a man knowing he had a terminal disease. I used to think you were a smart girl. But I take back what I said about this not being your territory. You'll like it here, so enjoy the scene."

She glared at him. "May I go now, Dr. Raymond?" she asked coldly.

He was crumpling the letter of introduction, and she watched him drop it carelessly into the waste basket. Then he looked at her again.

"I'll see you at dinner," he said. "There's one thing, though. You've come to the right place to forget. All tensions fade away on the good ship *Nirvana*. It's the same every cruise, with everyone finding a beatific oblivion for care, pain, memories, failures, and reality. They call it having fun, and it's the in-thing on the S.S. *Nirvana*. . . ."

He was lighting a cigarette as she closed the door, and back in her own cabin she sat on the bunk and discovered that she was trembling, and close to tears.

## CHAPTER TWO

Lindy was stretched out on her sofa reading a book when the third member of the nursing team, Sue Bainbridge, a slim blonde with blue eyes and a pretty, vivacious smile came hurrying in.

Sue had appeared at dinner the previous night, bubbling over with anecdotes of her leave spent in San Diego. Her arrival had enlivened what would otherwise have been an anxious meal for Lindy Madison, with Peter Raymond absorbed in Beth Kent, and her table partner, one of the junior engineers, as high as Peter and far less coherent. The captain had been ashore, and with no passengers aboard, the mood at dinner had been that of a reunion party. Lindy had felt a bit lonely and nervous—somehow out of it all.

She liked Sue Bainbridge. Sue had confessed jokingly that she was a ship's nurse because she hated the hard work and discipline of hospitals ashore. Sue might prove an indifferent nurse, but you knew where you stood with her. And her scatterbrained attitude toward life was certainly amusing.

"Hi!" she cried, breezing into Lindy's cabin. "Beth said she hadn't seen you around. I thought you might be in here. She just relieved me, so I came right up. Didn't you say you'd never been to sea before?"

Lindy smiled and sat up. "This is the first time ever."

"Well, don't you want to see the ship sail? We cast off in ten minutes, you know. And it's quite a thrill the first time; a regular circus."

"I looked out before, but wasn't sure if we could go out there with so many passengers at the rail, and. . . ."

"In this company a nurse is an officer. Peter or Beth should've told you that. Put on a uniform quickly. There's nothing to do in the office right now. This cruise is going to be a breeze. Only two diabetics checked in this morning.

Sometimes we have a dozen or more on insulin. Don't you have anyone to see you off?"

"My folks are in Los Angeles," Lindy said, slipping into her uniform.

"Mine are in San Diego. Mission Bay. You know it?"

"I've surfed there."

"You ride a board?"

Lindy laughed. "I'm just a body-surfer, I'm afraid."

"I could teach you when we get to Hawaii. Body surfing is okay—but just wait till you can ride a board. It's super! Anyway, you're way ahead of Beth Kent. She's a girl who never gets her bikini or her precious hairdo wet. Peter's a surfer of course, and Harry Kaine, the guy sitting next to you last night at dinner, is an expert. He's been promoted to third engineer this trip, so he was celebrating last night. He's married, but you have to watch him. That goes for most of the ship's officers. The young ones, anyway."

She was still chattering as Lindy adjusted her makeup and followed her outside. A band was playing, and the sound of excited voices swelled as Sue Bainbridge led her out onto the boat deck.

"These cruises aren't like ordinary passenger runs," Sue confided. "Three hundred and fifty passengers on the list. Works out at almost one crew member for each passenger, so we'll find a place along the rail. Look! There's a gap! Come on. . . ."

A network of colored streamers rippled in the breeze between ship and dock. The dockside was crowded with people staring up at the passengers lining the rails. Everyone was holding tightly to the tenuous streamers that had suddenly become the only remaining link between them.

"Sailing is always so exciting," Sue said. She reached out and caught a streamer someone had thrown up from the dock, and passed it to Lindy. "Here, hold this. They're casting off, and. . . ."

The blare of the ship's horn drowned her words and the music of the band. Lindy searched the crowd, trying to find who held the other end of the streamer but found it impossible to discover in the tangle of colors below.

A tugboat nudged the ship, and beneath her feet she could feel the slow stirring of the engines, like a giant awakening from sleep.

"We're off!" Sue shrieked. "Isn't it a thrill, Lindy? You don't mind me calling you that, do you?"

Lindy shook her head silently. The streamer in her hand was tightening as the ship began to move and the dock glided slowly past. For some reason she couldn't understand, Lindy found herself clinging desperately to the streamer. At the point of breaking, she saw a young man at the other end staring up at her and smiling. The streamer broke and he let his end fall and cupped his hands to his mouth.

"Bon voyage!" he shouted to her.

Lindy waved acknowledgement, but she could no longer see his face for her eyes had blurred with tears.

"It gets to you, doesn't it?" Sue murmured sympathetically. "Of course, it's worse the first time. Like you're really going to the other end of the world, and leaving everything you've known behind."

Lindy nodded. Sue was right. That was the way she felt. Leaving everything behind. Roy, memories, everything. . . .

The waving figures on the wharf were already becoming smaller. "When they turn us, you'll see the Golden Gate," Sue informed her cheerfully. "And after the tugs cast us loose you'll start to feel the sea. Have you ever been seasick?"

"No, I haven't, but there could always be a first time. Do you get seasick, Sue?"

"Of course. If the weather's bad enough nearly everyone does. But they time these cruises for fair weather, so don't worry. You don't *have* to be sick just because it's your first time at sea. Just make up your mind you're not going to be, that's all there is to it. Anyway, most of these pampered passengers have spent a lot of time on cruise ships, so they're used to the sea. Let's go forward and watch the tugs cast off. . . ."

A small passing boat gave a cheerful whistle, and there were tiny whitecaps breaking against the yacht club breakwater as they passed. Standing beside Sue, Lindy stared beyond the Golden Gate Bridge at the bluest water she had ever seen. In the distance the Pacific looked as calm as a pond.

The tall buildings of San Francisco began to shrink and grow dim behind her. Blasé passengers were leaving the rail for the bars. She felt her first real stirrings of excitement, staring at the sea ahead. Whatever waited out there for her would be new and different.

"We're away!" Sue Bainbridge said, studying Lindy's face quizzically. "Pampered by luxury in the good old American tradition, we are about to explore the romantic South Seas." She giggled. "At least, that's what the brochures say! Now suppose you let me educate you a little on shipboard customs? The bars will be crowded right now, but we can sip something long and cold in my cabin while we talk. I've done my stint for today and, unless there's an emergency, you don't have any duties until after dinner."

Lindy agreed reluctantly. She had resolved not to become too closely involved with anyone aboard the *Nirvana*, but it was easier to ask someone bright and friendly like Sue about the things she needed to know than to ask either Peter Raymond or Beth.


With Sue's help she adjusted smoothly to the routine and customs of shipboard life. Its rules, though few, had to be strictly observed, but as a hospital nurse she accepted that as normal procedure. There were fewer restrictions and far more freedom than she had ever known in hospitals.

As the ship glided across the calm blue sea toward Hawaii beneath a rapidly warming sun, Lindy unobtrusively took charge of the nursing side of the ship's hospital. It began to run more efficiently. Sue Bainbridge, she discovered, was a good nurse but easily distracted, and rather lazy. She had to be told to do routine chores that most nurses carried out on their own initiative. But she only had to speak to Sue tactfully and she would respond cheerfully and well.

Lindy knew that it was the environment that was to blame for Sue's lapses. There were times when she herself found it hard to concentrate on records and the endless pursuit of aseptic cleanliness. There were so many distractions beyond the open door. . . . But Sue began to improve, and that made the work easier.

Beth Kent, though, was a different proposition. Beth was a careless and indifferent nurse. If Beth could leave work for Sue or Lindy to do, she would. She was usually late when relieving either of the girls at the end of a shift. And when Lindy pointed out some omission, or reminded her of work she had neglected, she became sulky and defiant.

Beth had made up her mind to dislike her at their first meeting, Lindy knew, and she sensed there could be trouble before long. At first she thought Beth's dislike sprang from resentment that she had known Peter Raymond in Los Angeles. But she began to doubt that. Jealousy she could understand, but how could Beth be jealous of Peter when she flirted with every male who would look at her when Peter wasn't around? To be jealous, one had to be in love, and Beth was not in love with Peter Raymond, Lindy was sure of that.

Walking toward the hospital from the elevator, Lindy sighed. Peter Raymond had certainly changed from the sincere young man she had known, yet why should the change in him worry her so? After all it was really no concern of hers. She had hardly spoken to him since she had watched him crumple the letter of introduction and drop it in the waste basket. He had fixed working hours, and his morning and afternoon consultations occurred during the other girls' shifts. She only saw him alone in the hour after dinner, when he opened the office for evening patients.

When they met during the evening session and he needed to speak to her, Peter Raymond was abrupt, even rude. She wanted to think this was merely because it *was* evening, and he probably had a date. But it seemed to go deeper than that. And that was something she could not understand. It disturbed her with a vague sense of guilt, almost as though she was to blame for it.

On the system of rotating shifts she had worked out for the nurses, she was relieving Beth this evening. She would take over now until dinner, when the hospital would close for an hour since it held only empty beds.

Beth Kent looked up quickly as she came in, and the paper that she slid out of sight into a drawer was a magazine, not the drug list she should have been working on. She stood up quickly, eager to be gone. "I thought six was never coming," she said aggressively. "I hoped you'd be a little early. I want to go to the hairdresser."

"If you'd asked I would have come down earlier," Lindy said placatingly. "I wasn't doing anything special."

"Well, I wanted to, but I wasn't sure what you'd say if I asked."

"I would've said yes. Did you finish the drug list?"

"No. There wasn't time. There's a patient in the examination room. One of the deck stewards with abdominal pains. He thinks it's appendicitis, so I let him lie down in there while I called Peter . . . Dr. Raymond. I was just going to call him again when you came in. He isn't in his cabin."

She fumbled in one of the desk drawers and handed Lindy a sheet of paper. She skimmed through the particulars, frowning. Five-five P.M. Almost an hour since the man had come in. Pain in the right lower quadrant of the abdomen. Nausea and vomiting reported during the previous night.

Lindy looked up. "You didn't check his pulse or temperature?"

"Dr. Raymond likes to examine his own patients." Beth's brown eyes gleamed triumphantly as she decided she had scored there. "May I go now, Miss Madison?"

"In a moment, Miss Kent. You didn't call Dr. Raymond over the intercom?"

"If you think I should do that just because the patient *thinks* he has appendicitis, I will. Do you want me to?"

The malicious gleam in her eyes angered Lindy, but she kept her control. She said quietly, "The particulars here are a little vague, aren't they? However, they do seem to agree with what the patient thinks he has. I'll see him first. If I think it's urgent, I'll have Dr. Raymond called."

"He doesn't like being called over the intercom if he's busy. Don't say I didn't warn you. Peter can be very disagreeable when he's annoyed."

"I've noticed that. However, he isn't here, and he doesn't have any cabin patients to attend to, so I don't see *how* he can be busy. You'd better keep your appointment with the hairdresser."

"Thank you, Miss Madison," Beth Kent murmured with mock politeness. "By the way, Peter walked past just before the patient came in. He was with Merle Burton, so they're probably still together someplace."

Walking through to the examination room,

Lindy remembered Merle Burton as a willowy, attractive redhead who sat at the captain's table. Sue had told her Merle was a divorcée, and as Sue put it, on the prowl again. She had also confided that the divorce settlement alone had been sufficient to keep Mrs. Burton in mink and diamonds for the rest of her life.

Sue was a fund of information where the passengers were concerned. Most of it, Lindy suspected, gleaned from the social columns of the magazines she read so avidly. The wealth and marital state of the male patients was Sue's specialty. Like Merle Burton, Sue was also on the prowl, but not for any casual affair with a ship's doctor. Sue's objective was to marry wealth.

Lindy's patient turned his head anxiously as she came in. He was lying on the examination-room couch. He was a small, sandy-haired man with bright blue eyes.

He groaned involuntarily as he started to say something, then drew up his right leg and pressed both hands to his stomach. "That other nurse gone?" he asked in a shaky voice. "She getting the doctor?"

"Dr. Raymond will be called if necessary. I want to be able to give him your temperature and pulse rate." She took a thermometer from the sterilizer and shook it down. She put her cool fingers on his pulse and looked at her watch. A very fast pulse. She entered it on the chart Beth Kent had started.

The chart noted that his age was twenty-five and his name was Samuel Prentice. She checked the thermometer. 100.5°.

"How long have you had this pain, Mr. Prentice?" she asked, frowning.

"Started just before I came aboard."

"Did you see a doctor ashore?"

"Why should I? We got a doctor here. Anyway, it wasn't so bad then. Only last night I started to vomit, and the pain got worse. Aren't you going to give me something for it, Miss?"

She opened his jacket and felt the lower right abdomen. Her fingers were gentle, but he winced. The muscles were defending the trouble spot with rigidity.

"You're new, aren't you?" he grunted.

"Yes," she admitted, and smiled at him reassuringly. "You're going to be all right, but I'm going to have Dr. Raymond examine you. I'm afraid I can't give you anything for the pain until the doctor sees you."

"I've got appendicitis, haven't I?"

"Doctor will have to decide that. It could be something less unpleasant. But I want you to lie still for me. Right?"

Back in the office she made her call quickly, and listened for the message to be relayed through the loudspeakers: "Dr. Raymond, you are needed in the sick bay. Dr. Raymond, report to the sick bay immediately. . . ."

Her anxiety grew as the slow minutes passed. She was about to ask for the call to be repeated when the desk phone rang. She picked it up quickly.

"This is the hospital. Miss Madison speaking."

"Oh, it's *you!*" She couldn't mistake that voice, or the resentment it held. "I thought Beth was on duty. What's the panic over there?"

"We have a possible admission with abdominal pain, Doctor," she said calmly. "I think you should see him."

"I suppose he thinks he has appendicitis?"

"Yes, Doctor, he does."

"Passenger?"

"No. It's a crewman, Doctor. Samuel Prentice, one of the deck stewards."

"What are his symptoms? Have you checked? He could be malingering."

"I don't think he's malingering. He has severe pain in the lower right quadrant of the abdomen. It started just before we left San Francisco, so he's had it for around forty-eight hours. He says he vomited last night. His temperature is 100.5, and his pulse rate 130."

"Muscle rigidity?"

"Hard as a board, Doctor, and very tender when touched."

"Forty-eight hours you said?"

"Or possibly more, Doctor."

"Oh *great!*" Peter Raymond said disgustedly. "And we're still two and a half days short of Hawaii! Why the hell didn't the fool report to a doctor before we left?"

She didn't answer that. Instead she said quietly, "Shall I tell him you're coming?"

As she put the phone down a woman's voice said something teasingly at the other end of the line. Merle Burton's voice, she supposed.

She managed to smile reassuringly at Prentice. "Doctor will be here in two or three minutes."

"You think he'll take it out, or wait till we hit Hawaii?"

She smiled at him. "You're way ahead of yourself," she told him cheerfully. "But if it is appendicitis and Doctor decides to operate, I wouldn't worry too much. The sea is smooth, and I happen to know that Dr. Raymond is a very fine surgeon."

"The way I've heard it, he's more a good-time Charley; here for the cruise," her patient muttered. "If he's such a good surgeon, why isn't he practicing his surgery where it's needed, ashore?"

"I worked with Dr. Raymond in Los Angeles. He was a fine surgeon then, and working on a ship isn't going to change that. You're lucky to have him on the *Nirvana* if you do need an operation."

Prentice grinned ruefully. "Okay, Miss! If you say so. I haven't really had much to do with Doc Raymond except routine crew checks. And about the only time I see him otherwise is in one of the bars or with some dame. Maybe I got the wrong impression."

Finally she heard brisk footsteps outside. "Here comes Doctor now. . . ."

Peter Raymond came in frowning, but at least this time there was no lipstick on his mouth.

"This is Samuel Prentice, Doctor," she said, handing him the chart.

He looked at it quickly, and nodded. "Where did the pain start, Prentice?"

"Well, it started near my navel, Doc. Then it seemed to move to the right side of my stomach, low down."

"Intermittent pain, or continual?"

"It goes on all the time, only every now and then it gets real bad."

"All right, let's take a look at you. Miss Madison says you told her it started before we left port. Now suppose you tell me about that. . . ."

Lindy moved in to help with the examination. He was still thorough, she realized quickly. He was still a good doctor. The temperature of her patient had risen slightly, the pulse was faster, and she suspected, weaker. She watched Peter Raymond conclude his examination and straighten slowly, frowning.

"The pain still there, Prentice?" he asked.

"It seems to be easing right now."

"You've got an appendix that has to be taken out."

Prentice let his breath out resignedly. "I figured that's what it was. I suppose it can't wait till we get to Hawaii?"

"It shouldn't have been allowed to wait until you came aboard. It has to come out as quickly as possible. And that means just as soon as Miss Madison and her nurses can prepare you. I need your permission, of course. You'll be put ashore in Hawaii for convalescence."

"Okay. . ." his patient sighed.

Dr. Raymond glanced at Lindy. "Call Miss Kent and Miss Brainbridge here immediately. You'll find a permission form in the desk. Fill it out, and have Mr. Prentice sign it. The other girls can get him ready. I'll need you to prepare the instruments and scrub in with me."

"Yes, Doctor," she murmured.

The loudspeakers were relaying the calls for her nurses, and she was filling out the permission form when Peter Raymond passed the desk. "This needs your signature too, Doctor," she reminded him quietly.

He nodded and slashed his signature where she indicated.

"Of all the fools!" he muttered bitterly. "He has typical appendicitis symptoms *before* he comes aboard, then waits two days before telling anyone about it! I suppose you realize it's about reached the point of rupture?"

"Yes, Doctor. That's why I had you called."

"Beth started his chart. What the hell was she doing from the time he came in until you took over?"

"Reading a magazine, and worrying about her hairdo for tonight," Lindy thought disgustedly. In defense of her nurse she said, "Miss Kent called you in your cabin, Doctor. Several times, she said. But you weren't there."

"I'm not supposed to be in my cabin all the time I'm not in here," he said testily. "Even a doctor is allowed some private life."

That wasn't worth answering, she decided. "Preoperative medication, Doctor?"

"Miss Bainbridge will give it. I'm entering it on the chart for her. He'll need massive antibiotic therapy. We're going to be damned lucky to get his confounded appendix out in one piece. Well there's one thing, we've got a good surgical armamentarium. I saw to that! Go get his signature and witness it. I'll have the instrument list ready when you get back."

She hesitated. "What about anesthesia, Doctor?"

His deep blue eyes studied her, cynically amused. "In an emergency, you could probably give a general anesthetic. You've seen it done often enough."

"In an emergency, I suppose I could. Under the surgeon's supervision. But. . . ." She had forced herself to speak calmly, hiding a sudden rush of fright.

He laughed abruptly and looked away. "I believe you would," he said in an admiring voice, "even though you'd be scared to death. But don't worry, Lindy. I prefer a spinal anesthetic for an appendectomy. I can handle *that* with a little help from one of the others."

She let her breath out quietly. "You're right, Doctor. I'd try if it was necessary, but I would be scared." Relief sounded in her voice, and he was grinning rather maliciously as she went out.

Going back to her patient with the permission form, she realized that he had called her Lindy, and that for a brief moment she had glimpsed something of the man she had once known.

The preparation went smoothly with Beth and Sue assisting. With her instruments, hemostats, and suture trays ready, Lindy waited as Peter Raymond inserted the long, thin needle into the spinal canal. Sue stood by the sphygmomanometer, watching closely for any fall in the patient's blood pressure in the danger period immediately after the anesthetic was given.

Waiting while the surgeon administered a pressor substance, Lindy realized that it had grown very quiet in the small operating room. The ship's engines seemed to be barely turning over. Passengers, she supposed, would be puzzling over the ship's slowing as the officers on the bridge kept the ship steady.

"How do you feel now, Prentice?" Peter Raymond said unexpectedly.

"I'm okay. The pain's stopped. I feel lightheaded, sort of pretty good at that. Like a little high maybe."

"That's the tranquillizer Miss Bainbridge gave you," he said cheerfully. "How's his pressure, Miss Bainbridge?"

"140, Doctor."

"That's good. Okay, Miss Kent. Turn him

over and start the gravitational dextrose." He glanced at Sue. "Help her, please, Miss Bainbridge."

Waiting with her sterile instruments ready, Lindy Madison watched Sue unobtrusively take over when Beth fumbled. The patient was turned, the straps fastened quickly, the sterile laparotomy towels tucked expertly into place, leaving the lower right quadrant of the abdomen exposed.

Peter Raymond nodded and Beth Kent started the drip of dextrose that would continue flowing into the vein of his patient's left forearm throughout the operation.

"Feel anything now?" the surgeon asked.

"My arm hurts. But not badly."

"That will stop in a moment."

"I've never had an anesthetic before. When are you going to put me out?"

Ignoring his question, the doctor asked, "Pressure again, Miss Bainbridge?"

Sue moved quickly back to check. "Still 140, Doctor." She placed her long slim fingers on the carotid artery of her patient's throat and then gave the pulse rate.

Peter Raymond nodded approval. "Can you move your left leg, Mr. Prentice?"

Lindy instinctively glanced down at the feet beneath the sheet. They remained immovable as Prentice said, "You kidding, Doc? I suppose you've got 'em strapped down like you have my arms."

"Can't fool you, eh? Okay. Wiggle the toes of your left foot." The toes hadn't moved either, Lindy knew. The spinal anesthetic was working now, and had rendered his lower body insensible, even though mind and speech were still active.

"How's that?" Prentice asked anxiously.

"That's fine. Quiet now for a few minutes while I make some minor adjustments here. Okay?"

"Right-oh, Doc."

"You comfortable? Straps not too tight?"

"I feel fine. Legs a bit numb, but I feel fine."

"Good. Close your eyes for a while if you want to. Or you can open them now and then and look at the clock. It's seven fifteen right now. Suppose you remind me when it's seven thirty. Then you can ask me about the anesthetic again. Okay?"

"Okay."

Peter Raymond nodded to her, and Lindy moved her instrument tray into place behind the anonymity of the screen that hid them both from the patient. Very briefly their eyes met and he smiled at her, pleased with the way the swab had come firmly and without hesitation into his hand.

He bent, swabbing the site of the gridiron incision he would make at McBurney's point. The forceps holding the swab dropped into the receptacle Beth held ready, and he held out his hand for the first scalpel.

Lindy Madison forgot all else then.

The operation had begun. . . .

## CHAPTER THREE

He had incised the skin, secured the bleeding points, and clipped towels to the wound edges. He exposed the muscle and cut between its fibers. Lindy handed him a hemostat and retractor, and as he parted the muscle he looked up at her quickly.

"I want you to move closer and hold these for me, Miss Madison," he said curtly.

"Yes Doctor . . ." she said uncertainly.

She moved as he directed, taking hold of the retractor and hemostat parting the muscle and its aponeurosis.

"Hold it more firmly!" he ordered roughly. "Open it."

She obeyed, using more strength. The pull of the muscle surprised her, and she felt a little sick. Compared to other operations she had seen, an appendectomy should not frighten her this way. She supposed it was her closeness to the wound. The angle here was different from the way a scrub nurse usually saw it.

"Good!" he said. She became aware that he had been studying her face above her mask. He looked down again. "Hold them just like that, that's good."

He reached past her for a depressor and inserted it gently beneath the opened muscle to protect the underlying tissues. He began to expose the peritoneum, the protective membrane enclosing the abdominal cavity. Lindy saw him pick up the peritoneum gently with dissecting forceps and shake it gently to disengage any clinging underlying tissues, then reach for the scalpel. A nick with the scalpel held almost flat cut through the membrane enough for him to insert two gloved fingers.

"Right," he grunted. "Take those away. We'll have the next one on the line. I want you to hold it for me."

"Yes, Doctor. . . ."

Next in line was the retractor. She gave it to him, and watched him place it on her side of the table. Working it beneath both the incised peritoneum and the outer tissues, he drew it up and held it there.

"Get a firm hold, and keep it steady. Got it? No, lift harder and draw it toward you. That's better. Hold it there. . . ."

He peered into the wound, and grunted.

"About the way we thought. You'll have to help me now."

He had reached across quickly for a lint abdominal pack. He bent over, picking up the cecum with it and drawing it gently out toward him and upward.

"Hold this. I don't want it flipping back in at the wrong moment. Right?"

The tissue she held felt spongy beneath the saline-dampened lint. It was like holding a fold of elastic out of the wound, and it was slippery and hard to hold. Her lips drew together beneath her mask and she frowned, but she held it.

"Fine," he said.

She could see the inflamed appendix plainly now, swollen and reddish on the wall of the cecum, the network of veins upon it engorged by the infection.

"Won't it work, Doc? Maybe you need a mechanic, eh?" Prentice said in an anxious voice.

"Time up yet?" Peter Raymond asked.

"No, Doc. You got ten minutes."

"I thought I told you to stay quiet till then?"

"Sorry, Doc." Peter Raymond had straightened as he spoke, and Prentice said in surprise, "Say, you're sweating!"

"It's hot under these lights, and you're not helping any by talking to me right now." He bent again, gesturing to Beth, who moved in with a towel and mopped his forehead.

"Sorry," Prentice muttered. "A guy can't see what you're doing from here. I just thought if it was something mechanical gone wrong . . . ?"

"I told you it was an adjustment, and it would take about fifteen minutes. Now will you be quiet?"

"Sure Doc, sure!"

Lindy became aware of Peter Raymond's eyes studying her again.

"You'd better hold it steady," he said grimly. "No matter how your fingers cramp." Reaching for the suture table his face was close to hers, and she saw that his eyes were smiling above his mask. She looked away. When she looked down again, he had dissected the appendix from the meso-appendix holding it, and had stopped the bleeding. He was staring down at the appendix grimly, and she suspected it must be friable and very close to rupture. He was encircling it gently with toothless forceps before he ligated it. The care he was taking was a measure of the danger to their patient from a sudden flood of pus. He crushed the base and then ligated it.

Another pair of forceps went on, above the first, and a long pair gripped the base of the appendix firmly just above the ligature. He held all three instruments easily in his left hand. He began to apply a pursestring suture, working smoothly and quickly with his right hand.

Their eyes met briefly, and he said cheerfully, "Well, we'll soon know if this is going to work, won't we."

"It will Doctor," she said involuntarily. "I'm sure it will."

He seemed to hesitate momentarily, then the scissors snipped once and his left hand was lifting clear of the operative field with the severed appendix still held intact in the grip of the three instruments.

When it was clear, he let his breath out audibly. "It worked," he said. "Now I can fasten this. But don't let go yet."

Watching him invert the stump and tuck it away safely into the folds of the cecum wall in the center of the pursestring suture, Lindy sighed. Watching him working so smoothly, absorbed by what he was doing, she was again seeing the man she had once known. A vastly different man from the Peter Raymond whose flippancy and cynicism annoyed her so much since she came on board.

The pursestring suture drew tight. The stump was gone, the surface of the cecum wall smooth, and the stitches barely visible. He glanced at her. "Let go now. Your fingers must be cramped."

He was tying the last suture as Prentice's anxious voice said querulously, "Doc, you said to tell you when it was seven thirty. Well, it's that right now."

He tied the suture and snipped the loose ends. He held out one hand for the dressing.

"Seven thirty already?" he asked in a surprised tone.

"Yeah, Doc. Isn't it time you put me to sleep and . . . got on with it? I mean, if you've got that thing adjusted like you said?"

"I've been thinking about that," Peter Raymond said. "I've decided not to put you to sleep, Prentice. How do you feel? Any pain?"

"Like I said, my left arm is pretty sore. That's all. I don't have that pain any more. Did you say you weren't going to put me to sleep?"

"That's what I said."

"Now hold it, Doc! I'm no hero, you know! Pain I don't like . . . !" His voice broke off. "Say! You mean . . . because the pain's stopped it doesn't have to come out? Not till Hawaii?"

"You aren't going to need an operation in Hawaii, Prentice." With the dressing in place, Peter Raymond came around the foot of the table and looked at the dextrose feeding into his patient's forearm. "Keep your left arm relaxed," he ordered. "I'm going to take this needle out, and put a small dressing on your arm instead. It may hurt coming out, but after that you're okay."

"Doc, I don't get it. I'm not sure I *want* to wait till we get to Hawaii. I mean, I got myself sort of ready for it now, and. . . ." He broke off and grunted. "You were right! That *hurt!*"

"It won't any more. Miss Bainbridge, how's his pressure?"

"Almost normal, Doctor."

"Good. Put a patch dressing on his arm when I swab it."

"Yes, Doctor."

"There. I guess that's about all. Put him to bed. A third of a grain of omnopon every six hours for three doses, starting when you get him settled down. I'll enter it on the chart. And the antibiotic therapy. Miss Kent, will you call the bridge? Tell the officer of the watch to pick up speed again, all clear now."

"Yes, Doctor."

"Thanks, Miss Madison. I'm glad you were around. You can clean up now."

Lindy withdrew her wheeled table as Sue came in to remove the laparatomy towels and cover Prentice with a sheet. She watched Peter Raymond walk around to look down at his patient, pulling off his gloves. She was glad it was over.

"Prentice," he said quietly. "I've got news for you. You had a badly infected appendix, and it was very close to rupture. But that isn't going to trouble you any more. It's out now and the wound is closed. The operation has been performed, Prentice. All you have to do now is keep still for a while, then convalesce."

Prentice was staring up at him disbelievingly. You mean. . . ? I don't believe it! But . . . I didn't *feel* a thing!"

Raymond grinned behind his mask. "We gave you what we call a spinal block. That is we anesthetized your lower body and abdomen so that you couldn't feel any pain."

"I'll be goddamned!"

The faint thump of the engines was starting again as the *Nirvana* picked up speed and continued on course.

Peter Raymond pulled down his mask and grinned at his patient. "I thought you'd realize what was happening when the ship slowed down, Prentice. I'm glad you didn't. You were a very good patient."

"All I could see from here was that goddamn bottle and tube," Prentice muttered. "I thought you were having trouble adjusting it. And you had me watching the clock. . . ."

The patient's incredulous voice faded as Lindy took away the instruments. Alone, she shook her head and frowned. She had seen the old Peter Raymond in there, but she was thinking that the transition would probably be brief, indeed. Before the night was over everyone on the ship would know about the operation and rumor would probably make it exciting, even glamorous.

Peter Raymond would be the center of attention tomorrow, flattered by women passengers like Merle Burton.

But she forced thought of Peter Raymond from her mind and went to work. They had more to do now, a patient to nurse tonight. She began to think out the shifts. Beth Kent, she decided, was going to be furious, but she was going to do her share tonight just like the others.


Her patient was sleeping heavily under sedation when Lindy finally left the sick bay. She was tired from the long day, and becoming hungry again, for she had only taken time out for a snack since the operation. It was after midnight when a resentful Beth Kent relieved her, and the dance in the South Seas Lounge that Beth had left so reluctantly was now really swinging. Lindy avoided the brightly lit lounge, seeking the rail and the quiet of the open sea.

The sea tonight was flooded with moonlight, and couples were walking the deck or standing along the rail, more interested in each other than in the moon silvering the water. Some had brought drinks from the dance and their voices and laughter sounded as she passed them.

She had almost reached the end of the deck when a woman's husky voice somewhere in the shadows said clearly, "Peter, don't be so modest! After all, an operation at sea is really something, isn't it? We all think it's just wonderful. Even Lady Bernice said so."

"Conditions favored me, and I had one very good nurse," Peter said. "Are you warm enough out here, Jan? We could go to the Tahitian Club for another drink. . . ."

"Oh, I've a much better idea than that," his companion laughed. "I need a wrap. Walk me down to my cabin and I'll fix you a drink. Wait till you try my specialty—I've named it Moon Shot, and. . . ."

Lindy walked more quickly as she recognized Peter's voice. As they began to move away she turned into a doorway, only to be suddenly approached by a stranger.

"Hello! Now I would say you're Miss Madison, and you're just coming from the ship's hospital after commandeering my date for tonight's dance. Now that sort of thing is bad for my image, and Beth was furious."

She tried to walk on, ignoring him, but he followed her into the passage. His voice hinted that he was laughing at her, and when she saw his face in the passage light, she realized this was so.

His hair was thick and blond, his eyes blue. He was about six feet tall, and in his early thirties still had the build of a college athlete. It was Shane Reinhart, she saw now—Shane Reinhart, whom Sue had described as a newspaper tycoon whose wealth and influence were fantastic. He was smiling at her quizzically, as though he knew exactly what she was going to reply.

She hesitated uncertainly. "I'm sorry Mr. Reinhart, but we have a patient who needs postoperative nursing. One of us has to stay with him day and night until we reach Hawaii. Since there are only three nurses, we are working in shifts."

"Not exactly the way Miss Kent put it," he chuckled. "Don't worry, Miss Madison, I've forgiven you. Beth always contrives to irritate me after the first hour or so in her company anyway. I was quite happy to walk out here and smoke a cigarette. But since you've deprived me of my date, how about joining me in the lounge for a drink?"

She smiled involuntarily. "Mr. Reinhart, I'm sorry! I'm tired. It's been a long, hard day."

"I'm being brushed off?" He raised his eyebrows at her humorously. "Now you're really deflating my ego. Don't you feel maybe because you've spoiled my night you *owe* me a little something? Like your company over a drink? And maybe one little dance?"

She resisted an impulse to giggle. "No, I don't really. You did say you were quite happy to smoke a cigarette outside."

"But that was before you came along."

"That makes a difference?"

"Quite a difference."

Momentarily she was tempted, but she shook her head. "I'm sorry, Mr. Reinhart. I really am exhausted."

"Just half an hour? Then you can go—with my gratitude. And no argument."

"No, really I must go now. Good night."

"Perhaps some other time?" he asked hopefully. "When you're not so tired?"

"Perhaps. . . ."

"We'll get together sometime—you'll see. Good night. . . ."

He was walking outside again as she turned the corner, his cigarette glowing in the breeze.

After that, each time she came into the dining room he smiled at her from the captain's table, where he sat with Jane Carmody and Sir Richard and Lady Bernice Moore. His smile was charming and she often caught him watching her, but as the days passed there were no more invitations from Shane Reinhart. Her relief, she admitted secretly, was not without pique.

But she had other things to occupy her mind. Suddenly there were more patients, and the diabetics needed daily attention. Prentice was making a good recovery, but it was slow and Peter Raymond decided to keep him in bed until the ship reached Hawaii. Then he would be taken ashore on a stretcher.

It was very early in the morning of arrival day when Lindy came out onto the promenade deck. She reasoned that the effects of last night's fancy-dress ball must account for the lack of passengers on deck.

Standing by the rail watching the peaks and ridges of the island of Oahu rise from the sea, she was suddenly aware of a woman standing a little distance from her.

"Good morning, Mrs. Carmody," she said, moving toward her.

As she said it she saw that the woman was crying, and that she wore a wrap over last night's costume. Tears had streaked her mascara, and glistened on her cheeks. Lindy turned away, embarrassed.

"Don't go. . . ."

"I didn't mean to intrude. . ." Lindy murmured guiltily.

"Don't mind me; it's stupid, I know, but the first sight of Oahu in the early morning usually makes me cry. It's a form of sentimentality."

"It's . . . very beautiful," Lindy said uncertainly. "I thought there'd be hordes of people out here. . . ."

"Is this the first time you've seen it?"

"Oh, yes." Lindy glanced at her uneasily. The tears were drying, and Jane Carmody was starting to smile.

Her smile was charming and Lindy smiled back at her. Jane Carmody was traveling alone,

Sue had told her. But Jane never lacked companionship, Lindy had noticed. She was tall, slim, and stately; a lovely mature woman in her early forties. Her blond hair was always perfectly groomed, her blue eyes full of gaiety.

The first day out she had assumed quite naturally the leadership of the gay set aboard that seemed the center of all social activity. If Lindy had thought about Jane Carmody at all before it had been as a vivacious, rather spoiled woman, indefatigable in her pursuit of pleasure and excitement. To find her here, alone and crying, had been quite a shock.

"The first time I saw Oahu I was young, and very naïve. I was celebrating graduation and marriage in the same year. I was on my honeymoon."

"That must have been . . . wonderful."

"Oh, it was. But people change. Marriages break up. That wasn't the reason I was crying just now. I've visited Hawaii many times since then."

"Is that Diamond Head on the left?"

"No, those are the heights above Makapuu, and beyond are the Koolau peaks. Diamond Head and Honolulu are on the other side of the island. It will be long after breakfast before you see Diamond Head. You're one of the nurses, aren't you?"

"Yes. Lindy Madison."

Blue eyes swept over her appreciatively, and Jane Carmody nodded. "Enjoy your first sight of Hawaii, Lindy. It's something you'll never forget. Aloha-land as they call it, where Polynesia holds out her charms for your enjoyment. At a price. Now if you'll excuse me . . . I'm tired and I must rest. . . ."

As she turned, Lindy saw her face more clearly, and stared at her, surprised. Beneath last night's makeup was a deathly pallor, and she grasped the rail to steady herself as she turned.

"Are you all right, Mrs. Carmody?" Lindy asked anxiously.

She smiled. "I'm tired, that's all. I seem to have become fonder of drinking than eating these days. Which makes my trouble self-inflicted, doesn't it? Two or three hours sleep, though, and I'll be able to face Honolulu. Excuse me. . . ."

She rested at the door, holding it for support while Lindy watched, restraining an impulse to hurry to her assistance. She straightened then and went inside. But she walked like a much older, and a very weary woman.

There was an air of expectancy in the dining room at breakfast as the ship neared Honolulu.

Later, in the hospital, Lindy heard music and voices as the tugs nudged the big liner into the dock. But by then she was preparing Prentice for the stretcher that would carry him ashore to where the ambulance that had been ordered should already be waiting.

People wearing leis of tropical flowers drifted past the open door of the ship's hospital, talking excitedly as they hurried to their cabins to prepare to go ashore. Peter Raymond came in to examine Prentice.

"How am I doing, Doc?" the steward asked anxiously.

"The wound has closed nicely now, Prentice, and there appear to be no complications. In fact, they'll probably tell me I should have put you back to work when we get to the hospital. You can put a dressing on now, Miss Madison. Oh, and I want you to ride with him in the ambulance. I'll see you at Reception. Are his papers ready? I'll check them if you put them on the desk. Oh, and get me some aspirin and a glass of water, please. I have a headache."

"Yes, Doctor."

As she went out Prentice was saying, "Doc, I guess I have to thank you for what you did for me. I'm grateful. I realize you saved my life."

"So the next time you feel ill, go see a doctor," he growled. "Don't wait till you're at sea. The next time you mightn't be as lucky."

Lindy had the papers ready when he came out. She watched him swallow the aspirin and drink half a glass of water.

"I needed that," he said, picking up the papers and glancing through them. "I was up late last night at the ball." He studied her face over the papers in his hand. "I didn't see you there."

"I didn't go, Doctor."

His eyes swept over her neat figure. "You should have gone. It was fun. In a hula outfit you wouldn't have been short of dancing partners. As I remember it you used to be keen on dancing once."

She looked away. "I haven't danced in a long time. I haven't felt like it."

"Living in the past, eh?" His blue eyes sharpened. "That isn't going to bring him back, Lindy. Or bring you any joy. You're wasting the best of your life. You have to learn to forget, and you'll do that quicker if you get with it. Believe me, I know."

"I . . .!" The way he said that surprised her. She broke off confused.

He grinned. "It's no business of mine, I know. I can't even begin to understand how you could have gotten involved with the guy in the first place. But you've got to start again somewhere, and Honolulu is as good a place as any. Suppose you let me show you the bright lights? We have three days. Enough time to look around and have quite a lot of fun. How about that, Lindy?"

"I promised Sue Bainbridge I'd go surfing with her. . ." She said uncertainly. "Thank you Peter, but. . . ."

"Okay," he said, his pleasant mood changing abruptly. He frowned. "Anyway, don't add one mistake to another. A girl like you wasn't meant to be a spinster, so have *some* guy show you the town. No doubt you'll find other volunteers. You might even get to like having fun again. Take these papers with you in the ambulance, and wait for me in Reception."

"Peter," she said quickly. "It isn't that I don't like you. It's just that I . . . don't get over things quickly. I. . . ."

"I know exactly how it is with you," he said curtly. "And what I said was good advice. It's time you scrapped some of those inhibitions and . . . mistaken loyalties of yours and remember that there's more to life than healing the sick, or being obsessed by memories of the dead."

He stalked out, leaving her fighting a rush of

emotion that brought tears of bitterness to her eyes.

She picked up the papers slowly and went back to her patient.

# CHAPTER FOUR

The crowd was dispersing from the wharf as Lindy followed the stretcher down to the ambulance. The dock and the dispersing crowd could have been in any harbor. But the clothing was different—grass skirts worn in the ceremonial welcome that Sue had told her was an integral part of docking.

Through the small window that gave access to the ambulance driver, Lindy glimpsed an occasional building as they sped through the city, and heard the light-hearted conversation of the driver and his assistant, who seemed to be treating the rapid transfer of Prentice to hospital as a joke.

She was relieved when the ambulance came to a stop. Except that there were more Oriental and Hawaiian faces among the neatly uniformed nurses and interns, she could have been back at the Los Angeles Medical Center.

Peter Raymond was already waiting, impatient to be away, and the formalities did not take long. She shook hands with Prentice and wished him luck. Peter was talking to the doctor as Prentice was wheeled away. She waited for him near the casualty reception desk, not sure what he would want her to do next.

As he came striding toward her, Lindy heard a vaguely familiar woman's voice say, "I have a letter for Dr. Ling. Could you tell me where I can find him please?"

"Do you have an appointment, madam?"

"My doctor in New York wrote to Dr. Ling. He is expecting me to call."

Lindy turned. She could not see the woman's face, but she was smartly dressed, and that tall, slender figure seemed as familiar as the voice.

"Try hematology, third floor, madam."

"I suppose you're going back to the ship?" Peter Raymond asked curtly behind her. "We're quite a long way from the dock. How will you get back?"

She glanced at him. "I hadn't thought about

that. I'll take a cab, I guess. Doctor, isn't that Mrs. Carmody at the inquiry desk?"

She turned her head, seeking that tall figure again. Raymond said, "I don't see her."

The woman who had stood there was gone, the elevator door that had been open was now closed.

"She was there. She must have taken the elevator." And in a hurry, she thought, frowning.

"If there was anything wrong with Jane Carmody, she'd come to me. Last night she was the life of the party. That woman has more health and energy than most women half her age. You must've been mistaken."

"I'm certain it was Mrs. Carmody," she said slowly. "But I didn't see her face. She turned away quickly just as I saw her. Almost as if. . . ."

"As if what?"

"As if she didn't want me to see her."

"Rubbish!" he said. "Jane Carmody isn't like that."

"I've a car outside. I'll drive you back to the ship. I have someone with me, but she won't mind. It's still too early for lunch."

Lindy followed him toward the entrance, frowning slightly. That had been Jane Carmody. She was sure of it. She was remembering suddenly the way Jane Carmody had looked this morning. So pale, so weak.

"The car's over here. Mrs. Burton ordered it."

Merle Burton was sitting in it, she saw as they walked toward a late-model convertible. Their eyes met and Lindy forced herself to smile. She couldn't blame Peter Raymond for being interested in Mrs. Burton. She had the milky skin that goes with titian hair and large velvety brown eyes.

She looked what she was, Lindy decided resentfully. A beautiful but spoiled woman, with too much money and time on her hands.

"Hello there." Her voice had a seductive quality that went with the way she was looking at Peter. "Dispose of your patient successfully?"

"We left him in good hands," Peter said. "They'll have him up tomorrow, but he won't be fit to leave with us."

"Too bad."

"Oh, he probably prefers it that way. One of our ships on the Pacific run will take him home. Have you met Miss Madison, Merle?"

"Not officially. Hello." Her brown eyes studied Lindy speculatively, almost challengingly.

"How d'you do, Mrs. Burton."

"Peter said that you assisted him at the operation."

"I just acted as scrub nurse. Miss Bainbridge and Miss Kent were there also."

"I can't imagine them doing anything beyond the call of duty. Are you lunching with us, Miss Madison?"

"Oh, no."

"You would have been welcome. It is your first time here, isn't it? Do you have someone to show you around?"

"I . . . haven't had a chance to plan anything yet, Mrs. Burton," Lindy murmured as she slid into the back seat and Peter closed the door.

Merle Burton studied her briefly and smiled. "Well, it shouldn't be difficult for you to find someone to take you around, ship's officers and male passengers being what they are."

"I don't think Miss Madison would like that, Merle," Peter Raymond said cynically. "Male company doesn't appeal to her any more. She prefers memories."

Lindy sat back, fighting tears as Merle Burton pressed the starter and the car slid out into the traffic. She drove expertly, but fast, and Peter Raymond sat beside her silently, as though what he had just said was something he had immediately regretted.

Ahead Lindy saw the bulk of the S.S. *Nirvana* rising above the low dockside buildings as they approached the pier. She got out quickly before Peter Raymond could move to open her door.

"Thank you, Mrs. Burton."

She had turned the corner before Merle Burton could reply. Ahead, the purser and another officer were walking toward her from the companionway, and she stopped instinctively to blink back the tears. Poised there she heard Merle Burton say coldly, "Why did you say such a cruel thing to her, Peter? Has she lost someone?"

Lindy began to walk away, her eyes clearing. It didn't matter what Peter Raymond or anyone else thought about her. She had every right to grieve. Perhaps she would get over it one day. But if she did, it would have to be because of something she felt, something as strong as her love for Roy had been.

On board again, she looked around for Sue but discovered she had gone off someplace, apparently forgetting what she had said about surfing. So Lindy gave a surprised Beth Kent the afternoon off, and settled down to write letters to her relatives.

But she found it difficult to write. Outside the sun was shining too brightly, and there were too many interesting things waiting for her to see. The realization made her restless and uneasy.

After dinner she went up to the promenade deck to look at the lights of the city. They proved too much for her, and when Sue returned soon afterward from her date, Lindy took a cab to the Ala Moana shopping center, across from Waikiki Beach, an area landscaped with tropical trees, floodlit fountains, and gardens.

The stores were closed, but she gazed at the window displays, planning a shopping spree for the next day.

When she finally returned to the ship and her cabin, she decided that Honolulu was garish but delightful. She had discovered also that it could be a very lonely place for a girl accompanied only by memories.

She was grateful when next day a contrite Sue Bainbridge sought her out and suggested surfing at Waikiki. Lindy had just returned from her shopping with a new flowered bikini, a bright towel and beach bag, and she was eager to use them.

The surf at Waikiki was flatter than surf she had known on California beaches, but the setting was superb. Long, slow waves rose from a calm sea, to roll in and break in shallows that seemed only yards from the smart hotels along the beachfront.

Lying on her towel beside Sue, she stared at

the dark bulk of Diamond Head and watched the board riders and outrigger canoes rise on the breakers and come surging in. She bodysurfed with Sue until she tired, then lay on the beach feeling the caressing warmth of the sun, glad that she still had a California suntan.

She had thought her new bikini daring, but beside Sue's it was prim. Sue confided that she had bought hers in Nouméa on an earlier cruise. How Sue could surf the energetic way she did and emerge with it still on completely baffled Lindy. But it was certainly an eye-catcher, and they were getting plenty of male attention, both in the water and on the beach. Sue obviously thrived on it. She would flirt atrociously with any presentable guy who looked at her, Lindy thought. And in her daring bikini that meant just about every male in visual range.

Lindy tired of the attention they were getting and dragged a reluctant Sue down the beach for an outrigger ride. The outriggers were fun, and safe enough, she realized, after the first wave or two.

"Wait till I get you on a board," Sue laughed as they walked back to their towels. "You'll think that was kid stuff. Hey, isn't that Shane Reinhart over there in the red swim trunks? Yes

. . . it is!" She raised her voice, delighted, "Hi Shane! Come over and visit."

"Oh, no!" Lindy muttered in dismay.

Sue glanced at her in surprise. "What's the matter? Don't you like Shane? He's fun, and easy enough to handle, if you're not interested."

Shane picked up his surfboard and towel and came over to the girls.

"Hi!" he said. "So this is where you two have been hiding."

"Who's *hiding?*" Sue asked, widening her blue eyes at him.

He laughed. "I haven't seen either of you since we docked. And where did you get that suntan, Lindy? Not on the *Nirvana*. You've avoided the pool all the way across. I was beginning to think you couldn't swim."

"Oh, we have sunlamps in the hospital of course," Sue retorted, giggling. "We use them all the time. There's nothing else for a nurse to do on board."

"I must drop in unexpectedly sometime," Shane Reinhart said, grinning. "Might be interesting. Can you ride a board, Lindy? Sue is quite a surfer, I've seen her perform."

Lindy smiled. He looked attractive in his swim trunks. His skin was tanned a deep, tropical brown, and his body seemed lighter, younger than when fully dressed.

"I've never tried board riding," Lindy admitted. "The suntan, such as it is, is Long Beach."

"I'm going to start her education after lunch," Sue said, rolling over lazily on the sand to look at him. "We'll rent a board and begin kindergarten lessons. She'll be okay once she gets her balance. She body-surfs well."

"Have you ever skied?" Shane asked Lindy.

He could have passed for Sue's brother, Lindy decided as their eyes met. He had blue eyes like Sue, and thick blond hair. Although he was over thirty, and according to Sue one of the wealthiest men in America, he could have been one of the surf bums from the California beaches.

"You mean on snow? Yes I have. I used to ski quite a lot before I became a nurse."

"Where?"

"Oh, Aspen, and of course in California."

"Then you and I have something in common!" He looked at Sue. "Did you hear what she said? She's a skier. I can have her riding a board before we leave Hawaii!"

Sue gave her a slightly jealous glance. "So what's skiing got to do with riding a board? Skiing and surfing are different scenes, poles apart."

Noticing her expression, Shane grinned. "That's where you're wrong, Sue. You ride a wave in much the same way a skier rides the snow slopes. It's like the skier's slalom when a good surfer comes in on a wave—he zigzags, changes position to take advantage of any slope the wave can offer. And all done by balance and the movement of feet and body. Because she's a skier, I can make a surfer of her in three days. Want to bet? And just because you're a surfer I could have you safely skiing down a snowy slope in the same time."

"Skiing isn't for me," Sue said disdainfully, moving her slim body into a more comfortable position on the warm sand. "If it was, I'd be a ski resort nurse, not a ship's nurse. Give me sun and surf and a building wave, and you can shiver all you want in the snow."

Shane winked mischievously at Lindy. "I started this suntan on the snowfields. But let's not argue that here. I've a better idea. Let's discuss it over lunch. Then I'll rent a couple of boards and we'll start right in proving my point. How about that?"

Sue said, "Well. . . ?" and looked speculatively at Lindy, her arched black brows drawing together slightly.

Lindy said hastily: "Thanks, but I did intend to go back to the ship when I came out of the surf, and. . . ."

"So what is there to do on that old tub that

Beth Kent can't take care of?" he demanded. He got up grinning, and stared down at them, hands on hips. "Didn't Plymouth tell you the passenger is always right? And besides, I happen to own quite a parcel of shares in Plymouth's shipping line. So don't you dare refuse me! On your feet, wenches! We're going to lunch. . . ."

He bent and scooped Sue up in his arms, spun her around, and set her on her feet. Lindy had started to get up hastily as he picked up Sue. But she was too slow. Scooped up, she found herself getting the same treatment.

His strength surprised her, and left her breathless and flushed as he set her down.

"Now you've made us both dizzy!" Sue giggled.

"Impossible. With you dizziness is a natural state, Sue Bainbridge," he declared. "Come on, let's go."

The small restaurant he took them to intrigued Lindy with its air of island informality. Barefoot people from the beach wandered in and out, some taking away snacks, others lunching at the bamboo tables, many still in swimming gear.

The food was delicious—surfing had made her hungrier than she had realized—and Shane was an entertaining table companion. He seemed to know everyone in the place, and called the waitresses by their first names.

Lindy listened to Sue's bright chatter and Shane's comments on Honolulu and its people. At first she was with them, but not part of it. Then insidiously she began to find herself drawn into the conversation and enjoying it. She was sorry when the meal ended and they went back to the bright sun and the beach, where Shane rented a board for each of them.

"Okay, Lindy," he said as they shed their beach coats. "This is where your education begins. A surf board, like skis, gives better results when you wax it." He tossed her wax, grinning. "Just watch Sue and me wax our boards. Then you begin on yours. Okay?"

She caught on quickly—as she had when she learned to ski. Things like that always seemed to come easily to her. With the board waxed, she carried it awkwardly down the beach and pushed out between them for her first lesson.

The first incoming wave she encountered spilled her off and she lost her board. He was a demanding teacher, she discovered quickly. He made her paddle until her shoulder and back muscles were aching. By then Sue had tired of the session and was riding in and paddling out again beside a red-haired boy in green trunks who had seemed to gravitate to her immediately when she dropped out of the teaching threesome.

Many times Shane exasperated Lindy. She swallowed more salt water than she had in years, and her first attempts to come back to the beach were laughable and ended monotonously in disaster. But then slowly she began to catch on. And he was right. Once she started to get the feel of it, it was not unlike skiing.

And then late in the afternoon she suddenly did everything right and rode a wave perfectly right in to the beach.

As she stepped off the board in shallow water, her first thought was to paddle out at once and do it again. But unexpectedly her weary knees buckled and she fell in a kneeling position. Then before she could get up, a wave hit her from behind and sent her sprawling on her face. The backwash caught her and dragged her backward, panicking her momentarily until she heard Sue's laugher. Then someone caught her arm and helped her up; she saw it was Sue's young red-haired companion.

"You rode that one in like a champion," Sue giggled. "What happened then? Did you start to say your prayers? Shane must've forgotten to tell you, even in shallow water never turn your back on the sea. It sneaks up on you."

"My legs just got weak!" she panted indignantly. "It was all that paddling. I'm . . . *exhausted*. . . !"

She hadn't noticed Shane riding in, but there was a splash behind her as the surfer helped her wade out. Shane called to Sue triumphantly, "I told you she was a natural! Did you *see* that?"

"Sure I saw it. She did just fine. But afterward . . . I'm still laughing!"

"Hey, you're going the wrong way, Lindy," Shane protested as she dragged her tired feet up the beach. "I'll get the board. We'll try another. . . ."

Over my dead body we will! she thought indignantly. She muttered aloud, "Shane, I *can't!* I've . . . had it. I'm so tired I can hardly stand."

"It's always tough the first time. After that you don't notice it. Was it the paddling, Lindy?"

"*Was* it?" she cried indignantly. "I'm *dead!* Most of my muscles are aching, and I mean *aching!* Shane, it was good fun out there, but I'm through now . . ."

"Oh, well," Shane said philosophically, "there's always tomorrow. You can't stop now, you know. Not when you're catching on so quickly. Tell you what! I'll drive you both back to the ship. Have a good soak in a hot bath, and you'll be as good as new."

"I doubt it," she muttered pessimistically.

"You will. I'll bet if we had dinner somewhere here on Kalakaua Avenue this evening you could dance all night."

"And you'd bury me tomorrow," she said with feeling. "Thanks, Shane. It's been wonderful. But all I want right now is to put my feet up. Do you mind? I'll take a cab back. I don't want to spoil your fun, or Sue's."

"Nonsense. I'll drive you back. My car's parked near where we lunched. Want to come with us, Sue?"

Sue sighed. "I was beginning to think you'd forgotten I was here."

"I'd hardly do that," he said, studying Sue speculatively. Her brown body was lithe and beautiful. Her lips were full and red, and her eyes gleamed as she studied Shane's face as though taunting him about some secret thought they shared.

"Maybe you and I could get together tonight, while Lindy recovers?" he suggested. "And plan tomorrow."

She said throatily, "I'll think about that, Shane. Over a drink when we get back. I could use one."

He grinned. "Think as much as you like, so long as you say yes."

"Maybe I will. Even as second choice, it could be an interesting night."

"You can bet on it," he said triumphantly. "Suppose you two start walking while I take the boards back. You know where the car is."

Lindy's feet felt heavy in the soft sand as she walked up the beach beside a suddenly pensive Sue, and she was glad when they reached the car park. Shane caught up with them and opened the door, and she was able to sink back on the seat.

As he turned the rented convertible she glimpsed two beachboys riding boards effortlessly toward the beach, their dark bodies etched against a background wall of green water. She remembered how it had felt out there on that last ride, and the thought made her aching muscles much easier to bear.

The remaining days in Honolulu passed quickly for Lindy Madison. She had another learner's session with Shane and Sue at Waikiki, learning more quickly now. Halfway through she was riding waves that seemed smaller each day with the persisting calm. The small surf suited a beginner, and she did not care greatly when on the third day neither Shane nor Sue appeared. Their interest in each other after that first night had been obvious to Lindy. Sue had won Shane's attention, and she was making the most of her opportunity.

Lindy's muscles stopped aching, and her feet and legs were beginning to adjust to the mastery of board and wave. It was easier on the third day, when she bought a board of her own from a grinning Hawaiian salesman. It looked different from the one Shane had been hiring for her. The fin was sharper and of a different shape, and the board itself lighter and shorter.

The Hawaiian went to a lot of trouble choosing it for her, and afterward came down to the beach to explain tricks in its use that she doubted even Shane Reinhart could have taught her. She could feel the difference at once, and after a short time her performance drew admiring glances from beachboys and tourists alike.

And then, almost before Lindy realized, it was sailing day. She had missed the berthing, but she stayed on deck as the *Nirvana* sailed and watched the Hawaiian farewell, complete with band, hula girls, weeping, kissing, and singing.

Waikiki looked different from the sea. The waves she stared at now were in reverse—just rising and diminishing swells of green water with spume seen faintly whipping back from their crests, and an occasional surfer disappearing beyond. In memory she was back there riding a board, and . . .

She jumped as the ship blew a long, hooting farewell to Hawaii. Passengers wearing leis still crowded the deck rails, talking excitedly. She sighed and turned away, and saw Peter Raymond walking toward her with a lei in his hand. She moved instinctively to avoid him, then realized that he was looking at her steadily. She waited as he approached, remembering that she had hardly seen him since he had driven her back from the hospital to the ship their first day in Honolulu.

"For a moment there I thought you were going to run away from me," he said in a low voice.

"Why should I do that?"

"I can think of a reason," he said gruffly. "Look, I'm sorry about that crack I made when we dropped you at the pier. I don't know what made me say it. I was sorry afterward, believe me."

She frowned slightly, remembering. "Was there something you said that I should feel annoyed about?" she asked innocently. "I've forgotten."

He scowled past her at Waikiki, which was drifting left now as the ship moved toward Diamond Head. "I'd like to think you have, Lindy. But I doubt it. That's why you wanted to avoid me just now. Okay! I had no right to say it. And I'm sorry. I've been wanting to tell you that for the past couple of days. But you didn't seem to be aboard." He was studying her face suspiciously.

She smiled. "I don't remember seeing you aboard either."

"Mrs. Burton and I have been going places. And I guess you have, too."

"I've been learning to surf," she said coldly. "I enjoyed it."

"With Shane Reinhart?"

She nodded. "Why, yes. *And* Sue Bainbridge."

His scowl deepened. "You should keep clear of Reinhart. He's not your type."

"Oh? I'll mention that to Sue. She's the one who's interested in Shane, not me."

He looked relieved. "Sue can look after herself."

"But you don't think I can?" she flared, her eyes narrowing.

"If you want the truth, past performances do indicate that. But I didn't come here to fight with you. I came to give you this lei. Don't you know the old custom about throwing a lei into the sea as you pass Diamond Head? They say if it washes ashore on Waikiki you'll return one day and find love here."

"I have heard that, but find it hard to believe."

"Every now and then it does happen. People do find love in Hawaii. Here, let me put it on you. We're about to pass Diamond Head. When the others start, throw it in. Look down into the sea, the Hawaiians believe, and maybe you'll see his face. But don't throw it too late, or it will drift away and be lost, and your love with it, they say."

She allowed him to drape it around her neck. The musky scent of carnations filled her nostrils. The blooms were large and beautiful, and she looked down at them, pleasure overcoming her resentment.

When she looked up he had turned away and was striding toward the club lounge. She watched him go inside without looking back, and sighed and turned again to the rail. Some of the women were already taking off their leis and throwing them over the rail, bright loops of flowers bobbing on the waves as they drifted astern.

It was all nonsense of course, superstitious nonsense. Like throwing coins in a fountain or kissing the Blarney stone. But she removed the lei from her neck and threw it far out into the sea. It hit the water and began to bob bravely astern. She lost sight of it quickly among all the others now being thrown from different decks.

And as she stared down into the water, because this was what she wanted, she saw Roy's face very clearly, and she remembered what he had once said.

"I didn't want it this way, darling. I didn't plan it this way. But I love you, Lindy. I love you. . . ."

Her eyes filled with tears as she turned away slowly from the rail.

"Aloha Roy," she whispered, "aloha my darling. . . ."

## CHAPTER FIVE

There was a gay party in progress for the younger passengers in the Pool Lounge, with people cooling off every now and then in the pool. From the laughter, muffled shrieks, and occasional loud splashes, it was apparent to Lindy Madison as she tried to sleep that some of the swimmers had not gone in voluntarily.

It had been hot on deck, but in her air-conditioned cabin the temperature never changed. The noise from the pool kept her awake a long time and she was glad when it eventually grew silent and she could drift into sleep. But she had hardly closed her eyes, it seemed, when the phone beside her bed rang loudly.

She groped for it sleepily. "Miss Madison speaking."

A woman's voice said, "Oh, I asked for the duty nurse. Where are you?"

"I'm in my cabin, but on call. Who is speaking, please?"

"This is Mrs. Burton. I need your help."

"Are you ill?"

"No. It's Mrs. Carmody. She's lying ill on the floor in the reading room."

"I'll come down right away!"

"No, wait. She appears to be in a coma. Is she diabetic?" Merle Burton lowered her voice. "If she is, it could be insulin shock."

Lindy frowned, remembering the hospital in Honolulu and the woman who turned away from her quickly at the inquiry desk.

"If she is a diabetic, we have no record of that here. But if she has been on insulin, there should be needle marks."

"I can't see any, but she is obviously in a very deep coma, whatever the cause. This woman is close to death. You'll need a stretcher, and you'd better find Dr. Raymond as quickly as you can. I'll stay with her until help comes."

"Don't move her."

"I know better than to do that," Merle Burton said irritably. "I was a nurse before I married."

"I'm sorry, I didn't know. Do you know where Dr. Raymond is? Have you seen him tonight?"

"I saw him briefly at the pool with Miss Kent. I called his cabin before I called you but he wasn't there. Please hurry!"

The phone clicked as Merle Burton put it down. Lindy dialed again quickly.

"Miss Madison calling. This is an emergency. . . ."

As Lindy hurried into the reading room Merle Burton looked up quickly from where she knelt beside Jane Carmody.

"Did you find him?" she asked quickly.

"Yes, he's coming. And the stretcher."

"Her breathing stopped just after I called you. I started mouth-to-mouth resuscitation, and she began to breathe again. You're going to need oxygen."

"Miss Bainbridge is getting it ready in the hospital."

"Then you didn't lose any time. Well, I can find no signs of injury. And there are no needle marks. But check if you want."

She had wrapped Jane Carmody in a blanket obtained from one of the nearby cabins and had loosened her clothing to help her breathe. Lindy decided that if Merle Burton had once been a nurse, she must have been a good one.

"She was lucky someone with your experience found her, Mrs. Burton. And that you were able to give her mouth-to-mouth resuscitation. . . ." She broke off as she heard someone coming in. "Here's Dr. Raymond. . . ."

Merle Burton got up slowly as Peter Raymond came in, followed by two men with a stretcher. He knelt beside Mrs. Carmody at once.

"Does anyone know what happened? Did she fall?"

"She was lying right here when I found her," Merle Burton said coldly. "If she had a fall it left no bruises that I could find. I'd say she felt ill and headed for the armchair, but didn't quite make it. She collapsed where she is now."

"That's possible." He glanced at Lindy. "Anyone check for needle marks?"

Merle Burton said, "I did. Thoroughly. There aren't any."

"Does she have a handbag?" He glanced about. "There it is, behind that table. Miss Madison, see if there's anything in there that might help us. Barbiturates. Anything."

Lindy picked up the bag and searched through the jumbled contents quickly. "There's nothing like that, Doctor."

He did not answer. He was already examining Jane Carmody swiftly and efficiently. Lindy moved in to help him as Merle Burton said quietly, "You don't need me now. I'm going." She went out without looking back.

Lindy said in a low voice, "While I was contacting you, Mrs. Carmody's respiration failed."

"Failed? How do you know?"

"Mrs. Burton told me. She gave her mouth-to-mouth resuscitation until she began to breathe again."

He frowned. "Mrs. Burton has hidden qualities. We're going to need oxygen therapy—Mrs. Carmody isn't breathing well now."

"Miss Bainbridge will have it ready."

"Good!" He spared her an approving glance and stood up to nod at the waiting men with the stretcher. "We'll get her on the stretcher now. Lay it down beside her and I'll tell you what I want done." He looked back at Lindy, frowning. "This coma appears to be from a basic disease, and it isn't diabetes. I'm beginning to think it just might've been Jane Carmody you saw in the hospital."

"I was sure of it at the time." She hesitated, remembering. "Maybe because I'd seen Mrs. Carmody on deck early in the morning. She looked ghastly. We talked for a while and then when she started to leave she could hardly walk.

I asked her if she was all right, and she said it was just the ball the night before that had tired her."

"She said nothing else? Think hard."

"Well, she said it was self-inflicted. I offered to help her to her cabin—but she wouldn't let me."

"And at the inquiry desk, did you hear anything of what she said?"

"She said her own doctor had written to Dr. Ling, and that he was expecting her."

"Ling?" he said, scowling. "Ling? That name rings a bell, but I can't recall the association. Anything else?"

"She asked the girl at the desk where she could find Dr. Ling, and she told her to try the third floor. I think she said hematology."

"Blood disease? Well, there are such things as hematological comas. It could account for the anemia, which is obvious *and* severe. I'm going to need both you and Sue, and it could be a long night."

Peter Raymond was right; it proved a very long night, indeed. Lindy worked with him closely, with Sue hovering in the background ready to help when needed. They both knew they were watching the doctor fight for a woman's life, and it was long after sunrise before he began to win his battle against death.

Gradually, Jane Carmody's respiration and heartbeat strengthened, and her blood pressure began to rise to a more normal level.

They watched her slowly emerge from the coma into which she had lapsed. Her hands went up feebly to fight the life-giving mask, and she began muttering. A man's name, Lindy decided.

Peter Raymond moved in quickly to bend over her. "Did you hear what she said?"

"She was calling someone. The name sounded like Vern or Vernon."

"Her husband is Bernard Carmody, Doctor," Sue said quickly. "She was calling Bernard. They parted a few months ago. He was a big industrialist in. . . ."

He interrupted her with an angry glance. "I'm not interested in *that*. Miss Madison, you can take off the mask. She can do without it now."

"Mrs. Carmody. Can you hear me?"

Passing the mask to Sue, Lindy watched Jane Carmody's eyes flicker open slowly. She stared at Peter Raymond's face as though she could not see it clearly.

"Bernard?" she whispered. "Bernard?"

"This is Dr. Raymond, Mrs. Carmody. You became ill in the writing room and collapsed.

How do you feel now? Can you understand what I'm saying to you?"

Her eyes cleared slowly, focusing on his face. "It's you, Peter? Of course I can understand you. I must have fainted. I remember feeling ill and trying to get to my cabin to take a tablet. Then I tried to reach a chair in the writing room. I . . . I don't remember any more!"

"You collapsed, Mrs. Carmody," Peter Raymond said. "But you're going to be all right now. Tablets you said? Tablets your doctor prescribed? Then you've collapsed this way before?"

"This is the first time it happened, Peter. It was just a faint, I guess. As you say, I'll be all right now. I'll go back to my cabin and take a tablet and rest. Rest is what I need. I. . . ."

She tried to sit up but fell back weakly, with Peter Raymond easing her down. Perspiration from the effort beaded her lip, and her face was gray.

Peter Raymond said gently, "I think you should stay in here until I make a few tests, Mrs. Carmody. We need to know what caused you to black out like that, and then we can do something about it."

Her colorless lips formed a wry smile. "I must be weaker than I thought, but I'll feel better in a few minutes. You don't need to make any tests, Peter."

Peter Raymond's brows had drawn together as he studied her face. "It was not syncope, Mrs. Carmody. You were in a state of coma. And to help you, I need to know what caused it. Did your doctor prescribe the tablets you mentioned before?"

She hesitated, avoiding his eyes. "Why yes, he did. A course of them to cover the cruise."

"Are they for a heart condition?"

"My heart is quite sound." This time she managed to sit up and stay erect. Her smile seemed stronger. "Really, Peter, I'm not in the mood for guessing games right now. And I do prefer to rest in my own cabin. Heavens, you've seen enough of me on this cruise to know I'm healthy and active."

"I would have said so. . . ."

"So okay. Don't make me irritable by asking silly questions. The tablets are just to keep me going for the cruise. You know I play hard and burn up a lot of energy."

"So your doctor prescribed amphetamines, Benzedrine maybe? Is that it? I hope he also warned you that these drugs can be dangerous?"

"I'm not a fool, Peter. I take them as directed. Now if one of these girls will help me to my cabin?"

"*Was* it amphetamine, Mrs. Carmody?"

She hesitated. "I didn't ask the name of the drug."

"Then if you will give me the name of your doctor, I would like to contact him and find out."

Mrs. Carmody could become coldly determined, Lindy saw now. She said angrily, "You will *not*, Dr. Raymond. I'm grateful for what you did for me just now, but I know what I'm doing and I am not a drug addict, as you appear to think. Miss Madison, will you help me to my cabin please?"

"You're being foolish, Mrs. Carmody," Peter Raymond said quietly. "I can't *make* you stay in here, but as a doctor I'm advising you to remain while I carry out some simple tests. I would also like to consult your physician so that we can get at the cause of your trouble."

"As you said, you can't make me stay in here, Peter," she reminded him angrily. "And I don't have time for tests and consultations. Life is too short. I mean to enjoy this cruise." She looked at Lindy. "Are you going to help me?"

Lindy glanced at Peter Raymond, and he nodded. "Help Mrs. Carmody to her cabin, Miss

Madison. You needn't come back. Miss Kent can take over here. Let me know how Mrs. Carmody settles down."

The passengers were gathering for breakfast as Lindy Madison reached her cabin, kicked off her shoes, and sank wearily on the edge of her bunk to pick up the phone.

"Dr. Raymond?"

"I've been waiting for your call. How is she?" he asked.

"Sleeping now, Doctor."

"Did you give her one of those confounded tablets?"

"She took it herself. I had the impression she didn't want me to see them."

"I see! Any ideas about them?"

She hesitated. "They weren't barbiturates, and they weren't Benzedrine. I've handled too many not to recognize them at once."

The phone was silent for a moment before he said quietly, "Well, could you make a guess at what they were?"

"It's only a guess, but I think they might be one of the adrenocortical steroids."

"That leaves a pretty wide field of application if you happen to be right, doesn't it?" he muttered. "Adrenocortical steroids can be used as therapy to affect most of the vital processes."

"Yes, I realize that, Doctor. Do you expect a recurrence of what happened to her?"

"I'm damn sure of it," he growled. "We're going to see Mrs. Carmody in the hospital again very soon. And since she refuses to cooperate, what am I supposed to do? The next time it happens we may not be able to bring her out of it. I don't even know who her physician is, but thanks to you I *can* contact Dr. Ling in Honolulu. He must have the results of her previous tests in the letter she gave him. That letter should have been sent to *me*. She's my responsibility for the duration of the cruise. I'm going to call Ling."

"Yes, Doctor," she murmured wearily. She was putting the phone down when his voice, thinned by distance, said sharply, "Lindy!"

"Yes?"

"Thank you for what you did for Jane Carmody. Most of the time she's one of my favorite people."

"You should thank Mrs. Burton. Not me. Without Mrs. Burton's help she might have died."

"I'll keep that in mind, though I doubt that Merle would listen to any thanks of mine. We agreed to cut our losses back in Honolulu."

In favor of Beth Kent . . . ? Lindy thought,

and then the line was disconnected. She put the phone down slowly, and stretched out on the bunk, too tired to take off her uniform.

Almost at once she fell asleep. . . .

She wakened refreshed, then showered and changed while Helen Carter, the stewardess, brought her coffee and a snack.

"Don't know how you do it, Miss Madison," she said, pouring the coffee. "From what I heard, you all had a tough morning. Miss Bainbridge looked like she was hung over, and Miss Kent said she was *dead*. But you look great."

Lindy smiled. "They haven't worked in hospitals for a while; they've forgotten what it's like to be under real pressure."

"I guess that's it."

When Lindy had finished her snack, she went to the hospital to relieve Sue.

"Did you have a good sleep?" Sue asked as she appeared.

"Did I ever!"

"Peter didn't. And he's like a bear with a sore head. Keep clear of him if you can when he comes back. Oh, and he told me to get a bed ready for when Mrs. Carmody comes in. But there's no sign of her yet."

She glanced at Sue quickly. "Mrs. Carmody is ill again?"

"The way Peter put it, it isn't just *again*. She's been sick for some time."

"He didn't add anything to this morning's chart?"

"Nothing yet. He went to see her half an hour ago, and hasn't come back. She wasn't all that cooperative this morning, so maybe she doesn't want to come in."

"Quite likely," Lindy said slowly.

"There isn't much you can do for a sick person who doesn't want your help, is there?" Sue said disgustedly.

"If the trouble is serious, she'll come in."

"Sure! Like she did this morning, on a stretcher," Sue muttered wearily. "Well, I'm off. My turn to sleep, and how I can use it!"

Lindy was completing her paperwork at the desk when she heard Peter Raymond coming in. She looked up.

"Good evening, Doctor." She was remembering Sue Bainbridge's warning as she saw his face. He looked weary and irritable.

"It's been a hard day," he growled, groping in his pocket for cigarettes. "About Mrs. Carmody, Lindy."

"Yes?" A vague uneasiness stirred within her as his deep blue eyes studied her face.

He raised one hand and pushed back his

thick black hair. "She's coming in for therapy in the morning. She wasn't easy to convince, but she's coming in. Do you have her nursing notes from this morning? I'd like to fill in a few things."

"Yes, Doctor." She found the case history, with its attached notes, and brought them across to him.

When she sat down again, watching him nervously as he began to write, he said without looking up, "By the way—you were right about those tablets. It was one of the adrenocortical steroids."

"It was?"

"Yes, prednisone."

"Prednisone?" She remembered the drug, and a feeling of dread touched her. His eyes were avoiding hers now.

"Drug of choice with some terminal conditions. Four times as potent as hydrocortisone, and it can be given orally. She's been on it a month."

"Then you talked to Dr. Ling?" It did not sound like her voice. It was low but calm, although she didn't feel calm any more. Her mind was full of confused pictures she had been trying to forget.

"Yes, I talked to him," he said curtly. "Ling wanted to consult her own doctor before he would read the letter to me. That meant I had to call him twice, and it took time. He said her doctor had arranged for a second hospital check in Papeete, a third in Auckland, and so on. That was the way Jane wanted it. No fuss on the cruise. Nobody knowing."

Lindy hadn't answered. Her face, he saw, was very pale.

He said brusquely, "Do you understand what I'm saying?"

Her lips moved, but no sound came. She nodded.

"I asked Ling what the hell I was supposed to do about her between ports when, like this morning, she relapses badly. Finally he gave me the name of her doctor, and told me to call him in Los Angeles."

"In Los Angeles?" she whispered.

"Yes. I contacted him this afternoon. I told him what I suspected from a physical diagnosis without the aid of laboratory tests, and he admitted I was right. You must know her doctor, Dr. Jason Turnbull. Jane has acute leukemia, Lindy. And she knows it. Turnbull gave a prognosis of terminal three months from clinical onset, which was six weeks ago. Turnbull admitted that she can't see the cruise out. He tried to persuade her to stay in the hospital, but. . . ." He broke off. She was swaying in her chair. *"Lindy!"*

Sweat was beading cold on her forehead and upper lip. She felt the beginning of nausea, and then nothing. Peter Raymond leaped from his chair and caught her as she fell sideways.

He instinctively picked her up in his arms. For a tall girl she was lighter than he expected, and she looked very young and lovely cradled in his arms, with her head thrust back, revealing the smooth column of her throat and her closed eyes with long dark lashes.

Peter Raymond cursed softly, and it was himself that he was cursing as he carried her into the examination room and put her down gently on the couch. He loosened her clothing and opened the drug cabinet for a bottle of spirits of ammonia.

He raised her head. "Lindy!"

She inhaled and began to cough. Then she moved weakly in protest as the acrid spirits caught her breath.

"No. . . . ! No, *please!* I'm all right."

Her hands tried to push the bottle away, and he corked it and put it out of reach. He watched her gray eyes open slowly to stare at him.

"Feeling better?" he asked gruffly.

"I . . . fainted?"

"Out like a light," he said.

"How did I get here?" she demanded weakly.

"I carried you. You'd better rest for a while."

"I'll be all right," she muttered. She managed to sit up and shook her head when he moved to support her.

He was frowning down at her suddenly. "While we're in here alone there's something I have to say to you, Lindy. You fainted because something you've been trying to run away from has caught up with you. You're going to have to see a patient with terminal leukemia again, and you don't like that. Right now you hate me because I was the one to tell you about it. Now listen. I'm going to persuade Jane Carmody to go into the hospital in Papeete. But in the meantime she's going to need highly skilled nursing, and you're the one who is going to give it to her."

"I *couldn't!*" She was staring at him, horrified.

"You can and you will," he said coldly. "And maybe you'll thank me for it one day. But whether you thank me or hate me—you're going to do it. Understand?"

He had turned without giving her a chance to reply. She heard him put the nursing instruction sheet on her desk outside and leave.

She felt bitter tears welling up.

## CHAPTER SIX

The days dragged for Lindy Madison as she watched Jane Carmody change from a bright, vivacious woman to an invalid as the current relapse continued to weaken her. She was seeing Roy again each time she forced herself to take up her duties and nurse the sick woman. And each day was torture.

Roy's decline had taken long, slow months, but with Jane Carmody everything was cruelly accelerated. Lindy watched the anemia become profound, bringing the sickly yellow tinge of jaundice to her attractive face.

But like Roy, Jane Carmody had courage, Lindy discovered as the slow days passed with the ship steaming steadily toward Tahiti. She could still raise a smile each time Lindy came in, and she was patient while the more unpleasant nursing procedures necessary to keep her alive were carried out. Lindy never heard her complain.

She could feel sympathy for Jane Carmody, but try as she might, she could not overcome her dislike of being near the woman. She was being selfish, she knew. It was because each time she came near her patient she saw Roy again, and memories tortured her.

She found herself leaving procedures that she should have carried out herself to Beth or Sue. And afterward when she thought about it alone in her cabin, her guilt and confusion would increase.

It was inevitable, of course, that Beth would bring it maliciously to Peter Raymond's attention.

Two days out from the lovely island of Bora Bora, increased dosage of the prednisone began to bring one of those surprising remissions that she had seen from time to time in Roy. She recognized the signs at once as her patient's jaundice began to fade and her color and strength improved again. That as she knew only too well was the really cruel part. In a day or two Jane Carmody would be sitting out on deck in the sun again. Perhaps, as it had been with Roy, she would begin to move about, apparently as well as she had been during the first days of the cruise.

Until the next relapse came. Quicker this time, and even more severe. Perhaps . . . terminal.

When she thought of that, trying to sleep in her cabin, she knew that she would not have to witness it, and was relieved at the thought. In two days the *Nirvana* would reach Bora Bora, in three it would berth at Papeete, and Jane Carmody would walk off the ship and out of her life.

When she went into the sick bay next morning, Lindy heard Peter Raymond's laughter from the small ward, and managed to smile as she went in. Sue was in there with him, and she suspected that Sue had applied the makeup she could see on Jane Carmody's face. Sue had done a good job of it. With her improved color enhanced by the makeup, this was the Jane Carmody of the gay parties and dances in the ship's lounges.

Her eyes met Lindy's as she came in and she laughed delightedly. "See how much better I am this morning, Miss Madison? Marvelous, isn't it? Peter is going to let me sit on deck for a while tomorrow. What do you think of that?"

"Wonderful, Mrs. Carmody," she said smiling.

"Well, she deserves it," Peter Raymond said. "She's been a very good patient." He turned his head and looked at Lindy and his smile faded. "There's something I want to discuss with you before you take over." Once in the reception room, he continued.

"The way Mrs. Carmody is responding, we're going to have to break down the prednisone and the supportive therapy. We don't want her conditioned to the increased amounts."

Only that, she suspected with a feeling of apprehension, was not what he meant at all. His eyes had been cold and angry as he looked at her. More angry than ever before, she thought guiltily.

He looked at her coldly. "I think you know what I want to talk to you about."

"You said it was the therapy, Doctor . . ." she faltered.

"It's you," he said angrily. "It's your approach to this thing. The way you've been trying to avoid being in there any more than you have to. It's all wrong."

"If you want my resignation. . . ."

He cut her short with an angry gesture. "Maybe you'd like that. It would be an escape from something you want to avoid, wouldn't it? A nice, easy way of escape."

"I haven't consciously tried to avoid anything!" she flared.

"Maybe not consciously. Okay. But you have. Want me to give you instances? Instances where you left procedures to Beth or Sue? Procedures that you knew damned well I meant *you* to carry out?"

"If Beth Kent complained. . . ."

"That wasn't necessary. I've known exactly what you've been doing ever since I told you Jane Carmody had leukemia. And I don't like it! When your fiancé was at the Center, what kind of a nurse did he have?"

"He had . . . a special nurse of course . . ." she faltered, close to tears.

"Exactly. A senior nurse, capable of caring for someone with a terminal condition. The best available at the Center. And that's what you happen to be here. A highly skilled senior nurse with greater experience than anyone else. Do you think Jane Carmody deserves less? That she has less right to live out her remissions than your fiancé? I don't doubt that your fiancé was a fine man. I think I know you well enough to accept that you couldn't fall in love with less. But so is Jane Carmody a fine woman. I suggest you take time out from feeling sorry for yourself to get to know Jane better. It could be a rewarding experience."

"I like her," she muttered defensively. "I try to do the best I can for her. It's just that I can't. . . ." Her voice trailed.

"It's just that if there's a chance to escape, you take it. How would *you* have felt if the nurse at the Center felt the same way about him? If she had left it to someone with less skill, less nursing experience? Don't you realize that's exactly what you've been doing?"

"I told you that you can have my resignation. . . . !"

"Maybe you'd better read the fine print in your contract," he said disgustedly. "You're a ship's officer, signed on for the duration of the cruise. If you leave the ship before we get back to San Francisco you'll never nurse again. You'd better learn to rationalize this thing that's bugging you. Do you think you can nurse and not see leukemia again? It's on the increase and there's going to be a lot more of it before someone comes up with the answer. So stop running away and stand and face it if you want to stay a nurse. . . ."

He was going, but she couldn't see him through her tears. She found her desk and sat down, bending her head to hide them from his satisfaction. She slowly became aware that he was standing near the door looking back at her.

"You can do it," he said in an unexpectedly gentle voice. "I know you can! I know you, Lindy. Better settle down before you go in to her, people desperately ill sense trouble in others. Their condition sharpens their perception. . . ."

She might have tried to answer, but there was nothing left to say. He had said it all. He had laid bare the hidden problem in her mind.

But how could he know the way she really felt? Her doubts, her fears, her loss. . . .

She heard Sue coming out, and dabbed at her eyes quickly. But Sue had noticed, and was studying her sympathetically.

"Hey there! What is it, Lindy? Peter still in a bad mood? He tear a strip off you?"

"Quite . . . a strip," she admitted reluctantly.

"Ha!" Sue muttered disgustedly. "A guy who lives in his kind of glass house shouldn't throw stones! You're the best nurse he's ever had aboard, present company included. Look, if you'd like me to carry on for another hour, I don't mind."

Lindy managed to smile. "That was one of the things he was right about. I've been trying to run away from something I should face." Her glance at the closed door was involuntary.

Sue frowned. "Then that boy you were going to marry . . .? He had leukemia?"

Lindy nodded.

Sue came over and put an arm around her shoulders, studying her friend's face.

"Go and do something else for an hour! Anything! You'll feel better able to face it then. Honestly, I don't mind."

Lindy shook her head. It was worse when someone sympathized. She had found that out long ago. It was one of the reasons she was here.

"I *want* to help you, Lindy."

"I know," she managed to say. "I know you do, Sue. But he was right about one thing. If I want to keep on nursing, sooner or later I have to face it all again. It might as well be now."

"He said that? Why the . . .!" Words failed her as she saw the other girl's distress.

"No. He was right. I've known for quite a while this was the only answer. I just couldn't accept it, that's all."

Sue nodded sympathetically. "Anyway, Mrs. Carmody's having quite a remission, and it should last until Tahiti. I'd keep that in mind if I were you."

"I am." Only somewhere along the line there

would be another case when Jane Carmody was gone. Someplace, sometime, there would surely be another.

Jane Carmody was sitting up against her pillows with a fashion magazine open on her lap as Lindy came in. But momentarily, before she turned to smile at her, Lindy realized that she had been looking at something beyond the porthole that Lindy couldn't see.

"Oh, you've brought the orange juice," she said in a cheerful voice. "Thanks, Miss Madison. But I always prefer my orange juice with vodka. It brings out the flavor."

"And Dr. Raymond would have me thrown to the sharks if I gave it to you," Lindy answered smiling.

"I've known him to order it for me. Before I came in here of course. But never mind. I don't have any time to waste, though. What kind of day is on the other side of these four walls?"

"Perfect, Mrs. Carmody. Blue sea and sky for as far as you could see."

"I like that. I don't suppose you could arrange it so I could sit in that deckchair in the sun this afternoon?"

"Doctor wants you to build up your strength. He said tomorrow. But I'll ask him if you like."

"I wish you'd do that. Do you mind if I talk to you? It gets lonely in here, you know. And neither of the other girls interests me very much."

"I don't mind. But I'll have to keep on making notes while we talk. I am busy." She had said that last instinctively. It had been a part of her previous defenses.

"You'll find I'm starting quite a good remission. Almost as good as the one I was having when I came aboard."

"Better," Lindy said cheerfully.

"Better? That might be too much to expect." She studied Lindy's face, frowning suddenly. "You do know what's the matter with me, don't you? And that I'm . . . not going to get better?"

"You shouldn't say that, Mrs. Carmody," she murmured, confused. "You're so much better this morning that. . . ." But she could not quite go on with it; her voice faded.

"Oh, come on, Miss Madison! Let's not kid each other. I'm having another remission, that's all. That's fine, and I mean to cram as much living as I can into it, but a remission isn't recovery. And each remission is a little shorter than the previous one. We both know that." She smiled. "I have acute leukemia. Remember?"

"We . . . they don't know enough about it to be sure of anything!" She felt the warmth of anger in her face as she said it. "Do they know what causes it? Or why people get remissions? Or why sometimes, for no apparent reason, they are longer?"

"Or why sometimes it runs its course in a few days?" countered Jane Carmody, "without any remission at all? I've heard all the arguments. They're working on it. Any day now they'll find the cause. And when they find the cause, some genius will come up with a cure." She shook her head. "Maybe they will. But a little late to be of any use to me. Or are you asking me to hope for a miracle, Miss Madison?"

"Everyone hopes for a miracle. Why not?"

"You seem to feel very strongly about this. Have I touched a raw nerve? Did you too once hope for a miracle, Miss Madison?"

Lindy looked at her, startled. "What made you say that?"

"The way you looked and spoke just then." Jane Carmody laughed softly. "I'm beginning to think I owe you some kind of apology. When I first came in here I had the idea you disliked me. I was wrong. It wasn't me at all. It was this thing happening to me, wasn't it? It's taken someone from you. Someone you loved. I understand now."

"I. . . ." Lindy felt herself flush. She was remembering suddenly what Peter Raymond had said about the perception of the desperately ill becoming acute.

"I was right. You don't have to answer, Miss Madison. Forgive me. I won't speak of it again."

"It's all right."

Jane Carmody smiled. "No, it isn't. But I like you. I would like to talk to you sometimes, about other things."

"I think I'd like that too," Lindy said slowly.

"And maybe just leave the other as a . . . a sort of bond between us that neither of us really cares to discuss?"

She had asked it so wistfully that Lindy felt the smart of tears. She turned away quickly, entering the pulse and pressure on her nursing notes. "Why not?"

Jane Carmody sighed. "Maybe you don't know what you're letting yourself in for. My friends say I'm a feverish conversationalist. Once I start, I never know when to stop."

"What woman does? But I'll have to see that you don't tire yourself."

"Well, I'm all for that, since I mean to make the most of what I do have. I'm from Boston. Have you ever been in Boston?"

"I've never been East. My folks came from Denver, Colorado. When they died I went to live in Los Angeles with an aunt. I started nursing there."

"Denver? I know it well. My husband and I used to ski in Colorado—at Aspen."

"I learned to ski there too! While I was in high school. Franz Hurtz taught me. I used to go back there each winter vacation from Los Angeles Medical Center. I met my fiancé there. He used to ski before. . . ." She broke off abruptly, embarrassed. She had almost said, "Before the leukemia reached a terminal stage."

Jane Carmody was studying her face intently, as though she sensed what Lindy had withheld.

"Franz Hurtz? I used to have quite a crush on Franz. Bernard and I stopped going to Aspen three years ago when our marriage started to go on the rocks. I haven't felt like going back since. How is Franz these days? Still as charming and handsome as ever?"

Lindy smiled. "That's for sure. But I haven't been to Aspen myself for two years now."

"Franz will never change. He's a professional charmer, on skis or off. I imagine he'll be the same when he's sixty years old."

Lindy laughed. "I think so too! And now I'm afraid I'm going to have to make you rest, Mrs. Carmody."

"Whatever you say." Jane Carmody's intelligent blue eyes held a wistful expression as she added, "But you will gossip a little with me again later? About skiing, and Aspen? We seem to have something in common."

"I'd like that."

Jane Carmody sighed while Lindy rearranged the pillows. She settled back, smiling. "I'm beginning to understand you better, Miss Madison," she said quietly. "And I like what I'm discovering. It was this same horrible thing that took your fiancé from you, wasn't it?" She smiled when Lindy made no reply. "Your eyes admit it, so there's no need to answer in words. We've both lost something we value. A man's love. You couldn't help what happened. But with me it was through my own stupid vanity and selfishness. It wasn't until he had gone that I realized how much I loved my husband. Then suddenly there was this. He doesn't know about it, and he won't until it's over. He'd want to come back to me, you see. And I mightn't have the courage or strength to refuse him."

Lindy Madison was staring at her suddenly, appalled. "But surely. . . ."

Jane Carmody shook her head. "I've hurt him badly enough. I couldn't do that to him. And I suppose pride comes into it, if I'm to be honest. What woman would want to be seen by the man she loves the way I'll be when the remissions stop?"

"But if he loves you. . . ."

"No. I've thought the thing out, and this is the way I want it. He won't know till it's over, Miss Madison. And that way he'll soon forget."

Lindy was staring at her, dismayed. "But when you go into hospital in Tahiti, you'll be alone. You'll be lonely, and. . . ." She had almost said afraid. She added in confusion, "There must be someone you'd want to be with you. . . ."

"No. I was too selfish to give him the child he wanted. And there isn't anybody else that matters." She looked up at Lindy and smiled. "Please forgive me. I know how you must feel, having to nurse me. I'm not going ashore to any hospital in Tahiti, or anywhere else. I could have done *that* back home. I'm going to stay with this cruise for as long as I can. I intend to do all the foolish things I always have done while the remissions allow it. I'm going to go right on pretending that life is to enjoy, and that it goes on forever. Do you blame me?"

Lindy muttered something in her confusion and made her escape as quickly as she could, aware of Jane Carmody's curious eyes studying her reaction. "She can't do this to me," she thought in horror. "She *can't* . . . !"

The thought still dismayed her when the day ended and Beth Kent took over. Back in her cabin it was worse. She moved about restlessly until she could stand it no longer. She needed Sue's friendly companionship tonight.

She changed and freshened up and went in search of her friend. She walked across the foyer to the South Seas Lounge, but couldn't see Sue at the tables.

"Hi there!" Shane Reinhart was easing himself off one of the high barstools, a glass in his hand as he walked to meet her, smiling. "I was beginning to think you'd abandoned ship, it's been so long since we got together."

A lot of heads turned as he walked toward her. She could not see Sue.

"You were probably too busy to notice me," she parried. "Have you seen Sue?"

"Very little since Waikiki. We had a small disagreement. Sue sold her options in the news media in favor of oil." He studied her face admiringly. "Seeing you again convinces me I should've stuck to teaching surfing. Especially with such a promising pupil. Can I get you a drink? You are going to stay and visit, aren't you?"

"I was just looking for Sue," she murmured uncertainly.

"Something urgent?"

"No," she admitted. "It was just . . . something personal."

"Good! Then you'd better stay and visit. Even if only for a little while." He was leading her toward one of the tables, bending toward her confidentially. "She's out there in the moonlight. And she isn't alone. Her blue eyes are full of the reflection of oil wells, and the guy was positively drooling over her. Human nature being what it is, I'd say that by now Sue could be in his cabin studying color slides of his backyard gushers. You wouldn't want to disturb her dreams, would you?"

Lindy laughed. "Since you put it that way—how can I?"

"And you'll let me buy you a drink?"

"Just one."

"Good!" he said cheerfully. "I have a prescription designed expressly for nurses after a hard day. It's called Tahitian Zephyr. Tastes like ambrosia, but pleasantly lethal. I'm sure you'd love it."

She smiled. "I'd like to try it."

He nodded to one of the bar stewards, and offered her a cigarette. "Seriously," he said, "I'm glad you walked in. I have my moments of depression like everyone else. I was up to my ears in one when I looked around, and there you were. Suddenly everything was okay again."

He was having the same effect on her, Lindy decided, smiling. But she was too wise to admit it.

"Did your disagreement with Sue have anything to do with your gloom?"

He shrugged. "Only very slightly. I like Sue, and she's good fun to be with. But only on a casual basis. How's Jane Carmody today?"

"Dr. Raymond is pleased with her." She wished he hadn't brought up the subject of Jane Carmody. She had come here to forget that. Ice tinkled in the glass as she finished her drink, and he smiled and held up two fingers to the bar steward. It didn't seem worth arguing about, so the protest on her lips died.

"That's good news," he said. "The ship hasn't been the same since Jane became ill. She loves gaiety. She always has."

"You knew her before this cruise?"

"For years," he said. "And her husband. Now there's a marriage that should've seen the voyage out. No wonder guys like me take off when some beauty suggests wedding bells. We see what happens to our friends. Bernie was in love with her for keeps. And I would've said the same about Jane. But I was wrong about her."

"Why do you say that?" she asked, frowning.

"Oh, it was her fault," he said casually. "She was always too busy getting in the social columns to be around him much. London, Paris fashion shows, Florida—all that jazz. Bernie's business was in New York, and I guess he just couldn't keep up. The marriage began to crack a couple of years ago. They had a get-together in Los Angeles just before this cruise to discuss it. Jane is the kind of woman who attracts male interest all the time. She's never short of admirers. My guess is that she told Bernie something he didn't like to hear. Anyway, he walked out on her."

"It might not have been her fault," she said quickly.

He chuckled. "How you women stick together! Me, I don't care who was right, or wrong. I like 'em both. Anyway, Jane went into a private hospital in Los Angeles immediately afterward. Rumor suggested a nervous breakdown, as society likes to define the condition of people requiring a head-shrinker." Studying her indignation, he added hurriedly, "In Jane's case it must've been merely for psychological repairs after the emotional storm. Most of the time she's a particularly well-adjusted person."

Only it hadn't been any emotional storm that had put Jane Carmody in hospital, Lindy knew. It had been leukemia. . . .

"I think Mrs. Carmody is still in love with her husband, Shane," she said slowly.

He glanced at her sharply. "I'd like to believe that. What makes you think so?"

"Just . . . things she said. In confidence."

"Things you can't repeat, being a nurse? I see. I hope you're right, Lindy. Because if you are it will never come to a divorce. They'll get together again when the cruise is over. She'd only have to lift a finger and he'd come back to her."

She started to say something but couldn't go on with it. He stared at her, surprised.

"You're crying! Did I say something to upset you?"

"No . . ." she faltered. "You've been very kind, Shane, and I enjoyed your company." She stood up. "Please don't mind if I go now. I'm tired, and I have to see Dr. Raymond before I can call it a day."

He was frowning at her, his blue eyes sharpening.

"You're upset about Jane? That's it, isn't it? She's really ill? It's not just an emotional upset because her husband left her?"

He had spoken in a low voice, and she lowered hers instinctively. "I can't discuss Mrs. Carmody's illness with you. You know that."

He studied her face, frowning. "Bernard

Carmody has a right to know if she is seriously ill," he said impatiently. "I wasn't kidding when I told you how he feels about her. He'd want to be with her. He'd take the first plane and be waiting for us in Tahiti."

"I must go, Shane," she said in consternation. "Try to understand. I can't tell you anything about it."

"I'll speak to Raymond then," he said curtly.

"Mrs. Carmody is the only person who can tell you anything. Good night, Shane."

He frowned, perplexed. "Then Jane knows what she has? If it was really bad you wouldn't tell her. Is that what you're trying to say? You people seldom do. It's the old custom of keeping the patient ignorant so that they're easier to handle. Lindy, wait. . . ."

But she kept on going, and when she had crossed the room and glanced back covertly, he was stalking to the bar.

She let her breath out in relief. How had she gotten into that? She should have remembered that he was a newsman, used to wheedling things out of people, things they didn't want to discuss. If she had told him, he would have contacted Jane Carmody's husband. And if his judgment of the man was right, the Carmodys would have been reunited on the cruise. Jane

Carmody's last weeks of life would have been made happy ones. . . .

Perhaps it was the drinks that were making her feel like this. But someone should tell Bernard Carmody what was happening to his wife. . . . And tell him soon.

# CHAPTER SEVEN

The S.S. *Nirvana* had berthed, it seemed, almost at the foot of a green mountain that rose steeply from the sea to reach toward high, fleecy clouds. The loudspeakers informed the passengers that this was the island of Bora Bora and the jungle-clad mountain, Mount Otemanu.

Lindy Madison had brought Jane Carmody on deck earlier, and together they watched the ship glide through a gap in the reef into the mile wide, deep blue water of the lagoon.

"They call the entrance Teavanui Pass," Jane Carmody said, smiling as she watched the girl stare enthralled at the green shoreline.

"You are looking at one of the least spoiled islands of the South Seas. Some say the most beautiful. The town over there in the bay is called Vaitape. There's quite a good hotel, and some wonderful swimming, but no surf. The whole island is encircled by the coral reef."

"It must be one of the most beautiful places on earth!" Lindy said in an awed voice.

"Are you going ashore?"

"Do you want to be rid of me?" Lindy smiled. "I might this afternoon when Miss Bainbridge relieves me."

"Don't miss Bora Bora on my account. I'm going to tell Peter Raymond that I don't need as much nursing now. I'm doing fine. I'll be going ashore at Papeete. They're organizing a *tamaaraa* for the passengers. A feast complete with Polynesian earth ovens for cooking the pigs. And Tahitian dancing is worth seeing at a *tamaaraa*. At least men always think so. Especially if the wahines get at the wine, and they usually do. The dancing gets wilder and less inhibited as the night goes on."

Lindy smiled at her. "That should be quite an experience."

"Don't miss it. Hadn't you better go back to the hospital now? I heard Sue Bainbridge say Dr. Raymond wanted to see you."

"He'll be busy for a while yet. Is there anything else I can bring you?"

"If there is, I just have to call a steward. You're spoiling me. But I have to admit I like it. Probably because others have spoiled me for most of my life. But I told you about that."

Lindy Madison nodded. Jane Carmody had told her many things, and now a strong bond of affection was forming between them. It gave her the courage to say something that she had wanted to say for a long time.

"Yes, you did. Mrs. Carmody, I can't help thinking you're making a mistake about your husband. He should be told about your condition."

Jane Carmody frowned. "No. It would hurt him terribly. I've told you that. He'd want to join me here on the ship."

Shane Reinhart's words, she thought. "But deep down, isn't that what you really want? Isn't that the one thing that would help you face it? To have him here with you?"

"It isn't what *I* want that matters. Please don't talk about it!"

"But if he loves you, how will he feel when he finds out? What will he do? Have you thought of that?"

"That's over. He doesn't love me now. I said terrible things to him." She turned her head, and when she looked back a group of passengers was moving toward them.

"Jane, it's good to see you around again. The ship hasn't been the same without you," one of the women said.

"Are you going, Miss Madison? You always seem poised for flight each time we meet."

She hadn't noticed Shane Reinhart with them until he spoke.

"I'm wanted at the hospital, Mr. Reinhart," she said.

"Then Jane doesn't need a nurse. That's fine! Jane, you look wonderful. I'll bet in a few days you'll be dancing all night again, eh? I'll be back in ten minutes, and don't accept any dates while I'm away! Miss Madison, wait for me! I'm going your way."

He caught up with Lindy as she hesitated, and they left the promenade deck together. Glancing at him, she saw that he was frowning thoughtfully.

"So what I said when you let it slip that June knew what she had was right. Raymond wouldn't have told her if it was anything bad. And it's easy to see how much better she is this morning. She will be as good as ever in a few days, that's obvious. Which means I went off half-cocked about her husband. But it was the truth. He is mad about her. He always will be."

"I couldn't discuss her illness with you Shane, whatever you said. Not without her permission."

"Okay. I understand now, so there's no harm done. All the same, I'd like to see them get together again."

"So would I!" She said it involuntarily, and he looked at her quickly, surprised. She added hastily, "She deserves to be happy."

"So does he," he said. "Are you tempting me to play Cupid? Well, maybe it's not such a bad idea." The elevator had stopped, and he grinned at her. "Want me to walk to the hospital with you?"

"I think I can find the way, and Dr. Raymond is waiting for me."

"Lucky Raymond," he said. "Have you ever snorkeled?"

"What?" Her surprise made him chuckle.

"Put on goggles and a snorkel tube to explore the sea bed. There's not enough time to take you snorkeling in Bora Bora, but there will be in Tahiti. I taught you to ride a surfboard at Waikiki, and I intend to teach you to snorkel in Tahiti. If you put those gadgets on and swim over the coral reefs you can discover a wonderland. Want to be in it?"

"I'll think about it."

"So long as you say yes. Let me know in the Tahiti Club tonight. Promise?"

"Shane, I. . . ."

"Good girl!" he said. "I knew you would." He allowed the door to close and the elevator moved up again.

"But I didn't say . . ." she began.

She shook her head and smiled. He was sort of likeable. He grew on a girl. She forced a serious expression as she turned the corner and saw the open door of the hospital ahead.

She found Peter Raymond sitting at his desk staring down at Jane Carmody's case history.

"You wanted me, Doctor?"

He nodded. "Sit down, Lindy. There's something I have to tell you. I've done all I can to convince Jane Carmody that she should enter the hospital in Papeete. She refuses. That means she stays on the ship. There's nothing else I can do. I can't have her hospitalized against her will. I'm sorry, but that's the way it's going to be."

She said slowly, "It isn't unexpected. She told me that was the way she wanted it."

He looked up, surprised. "You're taking it better than I thought you would."

"Wasn't that the way you wanted me to? Face up to it?"

"That seemed best for you. Yes."

"You helped me to see that clearly. And you were right. Sooner or later I would have had to face it again. It might as well be now."

He nodded. "It will take courage, but you have that. I noticed you've been spending more time with Jane than you have to. She's becoming attached to you, dependent upon you rather than the others. She's been quite frank in telling me how much she likes you. And you? How do you feel about her now that you know her better?"

"I like her."

He frowned. "Don't allow yourself to become too deeply involved. I don't want you hurt."

She was avoiding his eyes suddenly, surprised by the tenderness she glimpsed in them.

"Just don't get hurt again," he repeated. "I'm glad that you came aboard. At first I wasn't. I didn't want to be reminded of the Center, of the might-have-beens. I had a lot of dreams in those days, Lindy. But afterward something happened. A door closed on me. A door I can't open again. Perhaps I'll tell you about it someday. I know you haven't liked what you've seen of me here. But it's the way I am now."

"I still see a good doctor, Peter. A highly skilled surgeon. I don't say you're wasted, but the scope here is limited for your skill as a surgeon. And no matter what happened to you, I can't believe you couldn't fight your way back if you wanted. You could have once, I know. So why not now?"

He shook his head. "I can't go back, Lindy. You don't know the facts."

"Even if you . . . did something wrong . . ." she protested. He interrupted her curtly.

"About Jane Carmody. I've decided to keep her on a hundred milligrams of prednisone daily, in four doses. I'm hoping it will give her another remission when she relapses. I contacted the hospital in Papeete, and they have mercaptopurine available. We're going to need that when the prednisone becomes ineffective. And we don't know how soon that may be."

"And after the mercaptopurine?"

"Something else. Probably amethopterin, but it's only rarely given a remission once the others have failed. After that there's nothing more we can do."

"There is something else we can do for her, Peter," she said. "She shouldn't be alone."

He looked up, frowning. "It's what she wants. I asked her about relatives. And she said there was nobody she wanted near her."

"She has a husband."

"They're separated. There's a divorce pending. What made you say that?"

"She's still in love with him. And Shane Reinhart says her husband is just as much in love with her. She sent him away deliberately, I think. It was to protect him. She doesn't want to upset him, to have him see what's happening to her."

"What does Reinhart have to do with this?" he demanded bleakly.

"He's known them both for years. He said he couldn't understand their breaking up."

"You didn't tell him that she . . ." he broke off. "No, you wouldn't. But even if Reinhart is right, what can we do about it? My instructions from her are to notify the next of kin in the event of death, but not for any other reason."

"*Somebody* should let him know!" She said it angrily. "If he loves her, he'd take the next plane and join her on the ship. Maybe at Tahiti! She'd have someone to cling to. Someone to comfort her. It's what she really wants, but she won't let herself admit it. And it's what he would want to do if he knew."

He was staring at her suddenly, angry and cynical again. "And you expect *me* to do this? To contact Carmody and tell him that his wife has terminal leukemia?" He asked it sarcastically.

"She must have given you his address as next of kin. All you have to do is call and tell him you think he should know. It will be up to him then, and out of your hands. And when he gets here and you see them together, you'll know I'm right. That you've done what's best for them both. Peter, please do it?"

He seemed to hesitate. "If there's one lesson I learned from what happened to me, it's that a doctor must live by the book of rules or get his fingers burned," he said grimly. "And that goes for nurses too. Jane Carmody has told me what she wants done. Despite her illness, she's quite capable of making her own decisions. Do you doubt that?"

"No, but. . . ."

"The wishes of a dying patient must be respected. Remember that. So unless she changes her mind, nobody from this hospital will contact her husband while she still lives. Is that clear?"

He had returned to his papers, ignoring her. She walked out onto the deck. The sun still shone, and on the promenade deck she knew that Jane Carmody would be holding court among her friends. Probably planning the activities of the Tahitian feast.

She walked slowly back to her cabin and closed the door. *Someone* had to contact Bernard Carmody. . . .

She began to think with affection of Shane

Reinhart. Shane had his faults, but he was not hard and unfeeling like Peter Raymond had become. Shane would do it. All she had to do was hint.

When she finally went in search of Jane Carmody, her deck chair was empty, and she had vanished with her friends. Lindy shrugged and reassured herself that Jane was not her responsibility today, since she was not on duty until the afternoon. She went ashore.

The stay at lovely Bora Bora was all too brief. The tranquil blue water of the lagoon, the white coral beaches, the tiny town nestling at the foot of green mountains receded as the S.S. *Nirvana* sailed the following day.

Jane Carmody returned to a familiar pattern once they were at sea again. Seemingly as gay and carefree as ever, she drank too much, and had to be watched to insure that she took her tablets. Freed from the confinement of the hospital, she seemed determined to leave none of her available energy unspent.

Other patients with minor troubles absorbed Lindy's attention, but Peter Raymond had allotted her the task of making sure Jane took her prednisone four times a day. Each time she gave Jane her tablets, Lindy found herself evaluating the signs of fatigue, and wondering, as she had wondered with Roy, how long. . . .

Most of Jane's gaiety was pretense, she knew. Courageous pretense. There was only one way she might be really happy for a little while. And that was with the man she loved.

The island of Moorea, facing Papeete across a quiet sea, was as beautiful as Bora Bora, and from a distance seemed as unspoiled, but Lindy was disappointed with Papeete. It seemed bare and brown and provincial, despite its background of green jungle. The waterfront was interesting, with French warships and sailors, hovering, giggling wahines, and the varied ships in the port, above which the white silhouette of the *Nirvana* towered.

Lindy bought herself a few things in the French shops—perfume, a dress, a beach towel —but suspected the prices were a tribute to the wealthy tourists on the American ship. Then Shane Reinhart introduced her to a different Tahiti, and the picture changed.

It started when he rented a dilapidated Citröen, and they bumped and squeaked a few miles out of town. The road circled the beaches, and she glimpsed native huts among the coconut palms, canoes, fishing on the reef, girls in bright print pareus, and naked children who waved at them.

Even the trees along the edge of the road were bright with flowers, and the air was perfumed and clean. The jungle started at the road and climbed the mountains beyond it, and toward the sea were palms and more flowers.

Shane turned off the road abruptly, following a winding trail toward the sea, and suddenly, as he braked, there was the beach before them.

The dazzling white coral sand was warm beneath their feet as they walked across it, Shane carrying the diving gear.

"Like it?" he asked, smiling.

"It's lovely, Shane."

"Good. See the green water on our left, about a hundred yards out? That's a coral bed, and the place where your education in snorkeling begins. Ever use flippers?"

"No."

"Then this I have to see," he grinned. "You'll wonder what's happened to your feet —until you get into the water. Then you'll understand why we use them."

He put on her mask, making a face at her through the window, then adjusted her buckles and flippers and put on his own gear.

"Today we're going to stay on the surface, so you won't get any coral cuts," he told her cheerfully. "But next time we'll wear wetsuits and go down."

He led the way down the beach, and she followed as best she could, shuffling along on her flippers. Her feet felt too heavy, and the flippers seemed huge. She began to trip and stumble.

"Help me," she wailed in consternation.

He shook his head, laughing at her awkward attempt to walk. "Not a chance. You've got to get used to them. Try lifting your feet higher."

She finally mastered it and followed him into the water. "Now show me how to use these things."

"There's nothing to show you. Just swim and see what happens. Follow me and take your time."

He swam as she had watched him swim at Waikiki, with a loose, lazy crawl that seemed as natural to him as breathing. She had no difficulty keeping up with him and was surprised at how easy it was to use the flippers.

"Where's that green water now? I can't see it," she called to him.

"Try looking down, and maybe you'll find it," he jeered. "No, not that way," he added hurriedly. "Put your face and mask under and breathe through the tube. Then just paddle around. Maybe you'll find Atlantis."

She ducked her head, and through the window of her mask she saw the bubbles and wavering streaks of amber light slowly become less active. Coming into focus, far down, was a submerged city of coral. An Atlantis of coral rising from the seabed in strange architectural shapes.

Enthralled, she stared at ivory minarets, purple domes of oriental palaces and churches, fragile pink steeples, blue spires, battlements, Gothic towers, bridges.

She lifted her head excitedly. "I saw it!" she cried. "I *saw* it! Atlantis, just like you said!"

Then he led her on a guided tour of the coral beds, showing her gardens of bright red fernlike coral wavering faintly in subdued light at greater depths. Flowerlike coral, open to the filtered sunlight, mushrooms of coral on giant stalks with heads as large as umbrellas. Gruesome shapes of gray, red, purple, yellow. Coral trees with amber branches where fish brighter than any bird flitted about.

She began to swim farther down with him, and there seemed no end to it. She felt that she could have gone on forever, but human strength had its limitations.

They swam back to the beach side by side, and he helped her take off her flippers and mask. "Well?" he asked eagerly as they sank down on the warm sand.

"I can't believe it!" she murmured. "It's something I dreamed. I'd have to see it again to believe it. But it won't be there tomorrow. It couldn't. . . ."

"It will be there for many years," he said.

"And then?"

He shrugged. "Then it dies. It loses color and shape, and crumbles into white sand."

"I don't want it to change; it's perfect!" she said, staring out to the reefs.

"You don't have to worry. It won't change in our time," he said with certainty. His tone changed as he studied her face, became more serious. "I spent a holiday in Tahiti two years ago and discovered this place. There's no village here, so the tourists don't come this far. It was hot. I went for a swim and happened to look down, and there it was. I couldn't believe it either at first."

"I wondered how you knew it so well," she murmured. She was not sure what made her ask, "Were you alone?"

"I had a date farther down the road. There's a good restaurant there. She was with another girl and a guy, and they'd gone on ahead. I stood her up. When I saw what I'd found out there, I think I forgot she existed. I remembered when I saw their car going back to Papeete; I was still in the water when they passed. They didn't see me."

"You should have shown her what you showed me."

"No."

"Why not?" she asked curiously.

He rolled over on his back with his fingers linked behind his head and stared up at the blue sky.

"We were all washed up, anyway. It didn't matter."

"Oh!"

He turned his head and looked at her slowly. "Do I sense disapproval?"

"Yes, you do."

"Suppose I told you that when a guy like me finds something as beautiful as you saw just now, he thinks this is *mine!* It makes him selfish. He doesn't want to share it."

"You just did. With me."

He nodded. "I've been wondering why. It's not my style. It isn't me."

She laughed uncertainly. "Don't sell yourself short, Shane! I'm beginning to think most of your cynicism is just pretense."

"Don't you believe it!" he growled. "I was educated in a tough school—newspapers! That makes for cynicism."

"I only know that out there over the coral you weren't like that. And no matter what you say, you seemed to want to share your Atlantis with me."

"I haven't mentioned it to anyone else before! So what caused this human weakness in me? Tell me that?"

"Maybe you're not as tough as you think?" she smiled.

He turned toward her. "I can find *only* one explanation, Lindy. I think I've fallen in love with you."

She was in his arms suddenly, feeling the warmth of his body against hers, the pressure of his demanding lips as he kissed her. She instinctively started to struggle, but he was releasing her abruptly.

"You don't feel the same way." It was a statement not a question.

"I . . . don't know, Shane," she whispered. "I . . . just don't know."

"There's someone else?"

"No. Not now."

"You mean there was, but you broke it off? Was it Raymond? Sue told me you knew him before this cruise. Then you met him again here." He added with an edge of bitterness. "Sue said Raymond had a crush on you."

"She must have been joking. We dated once, a long time ago. It wasn't Dr. Raymond, Shane. It was someone else. We were going to be married. He died, and it was as though the world ended for me. That's why I'm here."

"I see," he said slowly. He turned and found a cigarette pack in the pocket of his shorts, and offered it to her. She shook her head. "So, it's too soon?" he said, lighting one.

"Perhaps. I . . . don't know. How can one tell?" she murmured, embarrassed. "Shane, I think I'd like to go back now."

"Whatever you say." He got up with a lithe movement and held out a hand for her. She took it and he pulled her upright.

Her eyes met his, finding them sullen now and resentful. "Shane, it was wonderful out there, and it wasn't entirely because of the beauty I saw. A part of that was because you were with me." She hesitated, and looked past him at the sea. "Shane, I find this difficult to say, but I do like you. I like being with you. And I was flattered by what you said. I suppose every woman wants to be loved. But I would have to feel the same way, and I can't. Not yet. Not with . . . anyone."

In the silence that followed she heard the faint hum of motor scooters approaching along the road.

Somewhere in the distance a woman's voice called in English, "Where are you going?"

"Won't be long. I'll catch up!" a man replied. The sounds on the road above her passed by and began to fade.

"Are you sure, Lindy. Are you sure you don't feel the same way as I feel about you?"

He had put his hands lightly on her hips and was drawing her toward him.

"Shane, please don't," she murmured. "This doesn't prove anything."

"Perhaps it's just that you won't let yourself admit it. Oh, Lindy, you're so lovely!"

His kiss, his hands were gentle, but she began to feel the hunger in him, and its intensity frightened her, made her pull away from him.

"No, Shane!" she protested.

"Hello there!" a familiar voice said unexpectedly. "Everything okay here?"

She turned, red-faced. Peter Raymond was walking down the sand toward them. Beyond him she could see a motor scooter propped in the shade of a palm at the end of the path down from the road.

"It was—until you came along!" Shane Reinhart said angrily.

Peter Raymond was smiling, Lindy saw, but his eyes were cold and hostile as he looked at Shane. "I wasn't really asking you." He looked back at her. "Is everything all right, Lindy?"

"Yes, of course," she said quickly. "We were just leaving."

"Good. In that case, so will I."

"Now wait a minute, Raymond!" Shane said furiously. "You come barging in here, interfering. What the hell do you think I am? She's quite safe with me."

"Shane, don't!" she said quickly, frightened as he moved past her toward Peter Raymond.

Raymond backed away warily. He said quietly, "Okay. I just wanted to be sure, that's all."

Shane Reinhart's face had flushed. "I don't have to take this kind of impertinence from a discredited surgeon, lucky to still have his license!"

Afterward, Lindy was never quite sure what happened. But it seemed that Shane Reinhart had thrown a punch before he ended up on the sand, raising a hand to his mouth.

Peter Raymond was walking back toward the motor scooter. When he reached it, he kicked furiously at the starter and roared up the rough trail to the road without looking back.

"Shane, are you all right?" Lindy cried anxiously as she went down on her knees beside him.

"Sure!" he muttered. "Sure! Look, I'm sorry!"

There was blood at the corner of his mouth, and his lower lip was starting to swell.

"Let me see," she said gently.

"It's nothing. Look, I'm sorry it happened.

But I've got the kind of temper that doesn't like being pushed around."

"It wasn't your fault. He should've left us alone. You weren't hurting me."

"I wouldn't," he muttered. "No matter what. Believe that, Lindy."

"I know, Shane," she murmured soothingly. "I just got a little scared, and maybe he noticed."

"I suppose he thought he was doing the right thing," he admitted grudgingly.

"You shouldn't have said what you did. It was a terrible thing to say to a doctor."

He glanced at her quickly, frowning. "You don't think I would say that if it wasn't true?"

She sat back on her heels, startled. "Shane, it can't be!"

"So you don't know about it?" He studied her face, frowning. "He was involved in a road accident in New Jersey. A girl was badly injured. It was a lonely place and he took her to a farmhouse. He attempted mouth-to-mouth resuscitation while they called an ambulance. The farmer had to drive to the next farm to make the call because he didn't have a phone. Raymond was alone with the girl. He said afterward that her respiration and pulse failed and that she was clinically dead."

He hesitated, but she said, "Go on, Shane!"

"Well, he opened her chest with improvised instruments and massaged her heart. He had revived her when the ambulance arrived only a few minutes later. She started to respond, but died on the way to the hospital. The autopsy proved that her original injuries were not as severe as he had thought. The coroner suggested that she died as a result of the attempt to revive her. He gave an open verdict and suggested the medical board inquire into Raymond's conduct."

"Oh, no!" she whispered.

"He'd just arrived in New York from the West, as you probably know. He hadn't even taken up his new post. And the girl's father was a member of the board. He didn't take any part in the inquiry of course, but his influence was there. Raymond was a stranger and without much influence. They argued that the girl could have responded to resuscitation when the ambulance arrived, and that her original injuries should not have proved fatal. That was where I came into it."

She stared at him. "You?"

"I'm a newspaper man. Remember? I wasn't being altruistic to Raymond, I was just beating up a story. I started digging into it. The inquiry was being held behind closed doors, but we found contacts inside. The whole thing hinged on time—if she *was* clinically dead when he operated. Raymond swore she could not have survived until the ambulance got there, that brain damage would have been irreversible before that. But he was vague on time. His watch was smashed in the accident, so it was his opinion against theirs, and some of them were experts."

She shivered. She was now beginning to understand what had happened to Peter Raymond.

"What did your people do to help him?"

"Oh, we matched in print expert opinion for expert opinion. The thing dragged on. They began to get uneasy. They had about decided to take his license, but they changed their minds. Some of the things we said were starting to hurt. But they wouldn't agree that what he had done was right. There was still only his word that she had been clinically dead. They began to argue around the factor instead, and in the end came up with a severe reprimand. Which was about the same as giving him the ax anyway, so far as New York was concerned. The story died, and that was that. It wasn't big or important—except maybe in principle."

"And he came here?"

He nodded. "Surprised me when I found him aboard. He didn't know me, or that I knew him. Not until just now. I'm sorry about that."

"But he doesn't know you helped him!"

"And you'd better not tell him," he said grimly. "Or let him know I've told you all this. Dead stories are best forgotten. I only told you because you knew him before it happened."

She hesitated. "Shane, will you tell me something? Honestly?"

"Try me," he said.

"Do you think what he did was right?"

He nodded. "Yes. I knew he was right as he saw it, and this hasn't made me change my opinion. Maybe I'll apologize to him for what I said one of these days. Come on. Let's get out of here."

## CHAPTER EIGHT

Jane Carmody was back in hospital as the *Nirvana*'s siren hooted a melancholy farewell to Papeete while grass-skirted wahines waved and sang on the wharf. The town dropped behind, the white beaches of Moorea swam slowly past across the channel and fell behind, and Moorea too was in the past.

Lindy watched from the promenade deck with Shane as the ship sailed. She had spent a lot of time with him in Tahiti and knew that she would never forget the things they had shared as they went back several times to the quiet beach and the coral beds. There had been dances in the town too, and the *tamaaraa* where Jane Carmody had insisted they join her small but gay party. Lindy had eaten too much Tahitian food, and drunk too much French wine. She had gotten a little high, and Shane had kissed her passionately.

She was becoming more and more attracted to him as the long, sunlit days passed. He had a physical magnetism that she knew many women must have found irresistible. He was handsome and charming. And only occasionally now could she glimpse that other hard, cynical side to his nature that was his boast.

When she tried to analyze her feeling for Shane she could not. She was sure of only one thing—if what she had experienced for Roy had been love, this was not. Not yet. It did not have the same tenderness, the sympathy. She grew confused when she thought about it, as though she was being disloyal to Roy, and it made her feel guilty.

She seldom saw Peter Raymond outside of working hours now as her association with Shane took her more and more into the gay life the passengers led. Sometimes she saw him perched morosely on a barstool—alone, or drinking with a fellow officer. When he drank now he drank too much, but the occasions were less frequent.

He had taken to smoking a pipe, and sometimes she saw him leaning over the rail on the promenade deck staring across the sea. He was becoming a loner, content to avoid the company of others, and she knew why. It was because of what Shane had said to him at the beach.

When she looked at him and he avoided her eyes, she was sure he knew Shane had told her of the tragedy. She wanted to talk to him about it, to try to straighten him out about the way Shane felt. He needed a friend. He needed someone like herself who had known him before.

But each time she found the courage to make an approach, she sensed the waiting resentment, the inevitable snub, and could not bring herself to put her sympathetic thoughts into words. But like Shane's apology, one day she knew it had to happen. . . .

In the hospital he never faulted her work these days, but only when they both attended Jane Carmody were they close. It was because they shared the fight for her next remission, Lindy knew. And it was proving difficult to obtain.

Jane was rapidly losing her tolerance for the prednisone, and the increased dosage was now almost at danger level.

Jane had set her heart on being active again before the ship reached Samoa. There was a Samoan fire dancer she had a date with, she reminded them weakly but cheerfully, and American friends in Pago Pago always put on a gay house party when she arrived.

One morning, with Tahiti far behind, Peter Raymond was examining her while Lindy checked her blood pressure. She said quietly, "I'm much slower this time, aren't I?"

"A little," he said. "Ask me again tomorrow. I expect a change then. I think you'll be up and around by the time we drop anchor at Pago." He smiled at her. "Try not to burn yourself out as quickly this time, eh? You worry us."

"I worry me," she said. "Especially when I'm lying around like this. If it wasn't for Miss Madison, I'd jump over the side. I need someone to talk to."

"Indeed?" he said. "I don't find that very flattering, Jane."

"Oh, you!" she said. "*You* know too much about me! And you're not as bright as you were either, Peter. When you're in here you're just too professional, and outside all I see you doing is staring out to sea and puffing at your pipe. What's gotten into you, anyway?"

He frowned slightly. "Nothing."

"Well, you've changed. That's for sure. Maybe you should find yourself a nice girl like Miss Madison, and sign her up before it's too late."

He glanced at Lindy, and looked away. "She has other interests."

"Good for her! Now, are you sure I'm going to start feeling better tomorrow?"

"You'll feel the difference when you wake in the morning. I promise."

"Then I think I'd like to have a visitor today, if I may. That way, it isn't going to seem as long a wait."

"You may. For half an hour. Who do you have in mind?"

"Someone male and bright and flippant. I think I'd like to see Shane Reinhart."

"I'll make sure he knows you're holding court."

She gave him a weak smile. "Thank you, Peter." She hesitated.

"There's something else, Jane?"

"Just something I wanted to ask you. About these tablets. They're losing their effect, aren't they? Maybe this time they'll work, but what about next?"

"If that worries you, I do have other weapons in the armament."

"Each one stronger than the last?"

He looked away. "Why, yes, in a way. Though I'd prefer to think of it as more effective than the last."

Lindy busied herself quickly, hearing Peter Raymond go out quietly, and Jane Carmody sigh and lean back.

He was gone when she came out, and found instructions for her written on the sheet on her desk. There was a call to a sick child, Jan Calvert, in one of the lanai suites on the promenade deck. She noted the time on her pad. She knew the child had a temperature and that he was treating her in the suite on the parents' insistence. They had brought her nursemaid on the cruise, and although she seemed to love the child, it was obvious to Lindy she was quite inexperienced in matters of nursing.

Someone walked in, and when she looked up, Shane was smiling at her.

"Hi! How's my favorite nurse?" He came over to sit on the edge of her desk. "And what's this about Jane Carmody? Raymond said she would like to see me. How is she, Lindy?"

She glanced at Jan Calvert's sheet before her on the desk. "Her condition is satisfactory, Shane. She just wants to talk to someone, and she nominated you as bright enough to cheer her up."

"I'm flattered," he grinned. "Raymond said half an hour. Do I just walk in? I thought of bringing her some little thing, like chocolates, flowers, maybe a bottle of her favorite perfume. But I thought I should ask you first."

Lindy laughed. "She has plenty of flowers, Shane. And no doubt she'll punish her digestion enough in Samoa."

"You expect her to be up and about by then?"

"Dr. Raymond said so this morning. I'll take you in."

He frowned at her. "Funny. I've never known her to be this sick. Why now, Lindy? She didn't look well in Tahiti. Didn't seem to pick up after her last time in here. Is it the same trouble?"

She studied his face. He was worried about Jane Carmody. His expressive blue eyes revealed that plainly.

She said in a low voice, "You do like her, don't you, Shane?"

"I told you that. She's a grand person."

"Then cheer her up. Talk to her about . . . her husband. You know. You have something there that none of us can talk about."

He stared at her. "You think she might take him back?"

"I know she wants to," she said in a low voice. "She may not admit it, but that's how it is. Shane, if they are your friends, try to bring them together again. On this cruise."

"On this cruise? Is she *seriously* ill?"

"Shane, *please*. . .! Just talk to her, and form your own opinion. You're not bound by the same rules we are. You'll know what to do. You'll know what's best for them both."

"I see," he said slowly. "Then there *is* something . . . something neither you nor Raymond can speak about. Is this because she's forbidden you to speak of it? Or because of clichés Medicine calls its ethics?"

"Be tactful with her, Shane. I'll take you in now."

He shook his head, and followed her down the passage. She tapped on the door, and went in smiling. "Mrs. Carmody, Mr. Reinhart is here to see you."

"Hello, Shane. So you took pity on me." Lindy watched her face change, brighten, become vivacious again as she smiled.

"Pity?" he said, grinning as he sank into the chair, and took her hand in his. "I'm a committee of protest! While you're sulking down here the ship is like a morgue without you. You've been up and down like a yo-yo ever since Hawaii. Explain yourself, woman."

She was laughing as Lindy closed the door. She went back to her desk, but couldn't concentrate.

"It's done," she thought in sudden fright. "I've said it! Indirectly, but I've said it. And he will know what to do. He will let Bernard Carmody know she's ill. Nobody can stop Shane from doing that. Her husband will be here when. . . ."

It seemed a long time before Shane came out again, quietly closing the door behind him. He walked over to Lindy's desk and stood there, frowning.

"She went to sleep, so I came away. That's quite a change in her, and frankly, Lindy, it shocked me! It's as though all the strength and vitality has run out of her." He shook his head. "Jane is a sick woman."

"If you come back tomorrow you'll see her start to change again. She'll be a little brighter, a little stronger. You talked to her?"

"About Bernard, yes. She needs him and she's still fond of him, I'm sure of that. But she won't admit it. Just let me take it from here. Right?"

She put her hand on his and smiled at him. "Shane, you're an angel!"

"Don't say that where my public can hear

you. You'll spoil my image. Can I see you in the club tonight?"

"Same barstool," she smiled. "I'll be disappointed if you're not there."

"Just let anyone try to keep me away," he grinned. "Okay. I'll try to have some sort of little surprise for you. . . ."

When he had gone she went in to make Jane Carmody comfortable. She studied her patient's face sympathetically and saw it was thinner, the shadows beneath her eyes darker. The yellowish, jaundiced tinge of excessive anemia showed through the makeup.

She crept out quietly. Her patient was smiling as she slept, as though she still listened to Shane's cheerful voice. Shane had been good for her, Lindy decided as she closed the door. Shane would be good for any woman.


He was waiting for her when she entered the Tahitian Club. He glanced at his watch as she joined him, and pretended to scowl.

"How could you do this to me? Don't you know you're six minutes and seventeen and a half seconds late? I've something to show you." He took a paper from his pocket and put it in her hand. It was a telegram. She looked up at him, and he nodded. "Read it."

She unfolded the slip quickly.

"*Intend join ship Auckland. Stop B.C.*" she read.

She looked up at him slowly, her eyes filling with tears. She watched his smile fade.

"Hey there!" he muttered. "Is it really as bad as that? I suspected it when I saw her today, so I made my message pretty strong, but I hoped I was wrong. God! I think we both need a drink. Let's move to a corner table."

She nodded and let him take her arm. "I'm sorry, Shane. I've grown . . . fond of her. I don't usually do this. . . ."

"I know," he said. "Remember, when Bernard gets here you had nothing to do with it. Neither did Raymond, if anyone asks me. I visited her and formed my own opinion. We talked about her husband and old times for a while, and I decided he should be here. The fact that he agreed at once leaves my conscience clear, and if any goddamn busybody says otherwise they're in for trouble. Now let's not talk about it again."

"Okay . . ." she faltered.

"Good! What made you late?"

"I. . . ." She dabbed at her eyes, and managed to smile at him gratefully. "There's a sick child. And there was a little trouble up there."

"The Calvert kid? Cute but spoiled. Has a private nurse name of Francine Moore—brunette, but nothing upstairs. She's dating Third Officer Martin, when the Calverts let her off the leash."

Lindy shook her head. "Sometimes you make me dizzy!"

"Not as dizzy as Bob Martin says the brunette is. What was the trouble that delayed you?"

"The child has rheumatic fever, so the cruise isn't helping her any. She's having an attack, and Francine has been using a croup lamp to help her breathing."

"Someone should tell her that a naked flame aboard ship is against regulations."

"Dr. Raymond did. He also told the Calverts there was nothing wrong with the child's respiration that the lamp could help. It wasn't well received. The child cried for the lamp; she's probably become conditioned to it. Francine cried in sympathy and they said she was the best nurse they'd ever had and were quite satisfied with the way she was running things."

"For nurse read baby-sitter," he said, grinning. "I wonder what they'd say if I told them she takes Jan to her cabin at nights, while they're out, and entertains Bob Martin down there?"

She looked at him, startled. "She *doesn't?*"

"Bob Martin said so in a moment of inebriated confidence."

"Of all the . . ." she started to say indignantly.

"Shh!" he hissed. "You'd be surprised how the other half lives. Here come our drinks. What do you say we move on to the South Seas Lounge for some dancing? Brighten you up?"

"Well. . . ."

Time always passed quickly when she was with Shane.

In the hospital as the ship approached Samoa, Lindy watched the miracle of the remission she had helped Peter Raymond gain for their patient. She watched Jane Carmody strengthen and brighten. The color came back into her face as the jaundice passed and the anemia lessened. The prednisone dosage had been reduced to normal.

When the ship berthed at Pago Pago, she was back in circulation. Her friends came and immediately whisked her off to their home for a gay reunion.

Samoa reminded Lindy of Hawaii on a small scale. The harbor setting was lovely—the crater of an old volcano, one wall of which had slid obligingly down into the deep blue sea to allow entry. The harbor and cloud-wrapped Rainmaker Mountain were the principal features of the landscape, and soon after arrival the mountain began making rain.

But Shane was there, so the bad weather did not matter greatly. They visited American and Samoan restaurants, and were dancing every evening.

It was sailing day again, and as though the making of rain was really a prerogative of that towering old mountain, the *Nirvana* was no sooner out of sight of land than the clouds fell away and the sun shone. Relieved passengers filled the swimming pool once again.

When Lindy was off duty it had become a habit to look for Jane Carmody by the swimming pool, where she sunbathed daily with her friends.

As she walked onto the pool deck she noticed Peter Raymond sitting at one of the tables watching the crowd around the pool.

"Miss Madison!" he called, as he saw her.

"Yes, Doctor?"

He was standing up as she went over to him.

"I'd like to discuss something with you. It won't take long. Do you mind?"

"Not at all, Doctor."

"Can I get you a drink?" He held her chair as she sat down.

"No, thank you."

His pipe trailed thin blue smoke from the ashtray. He sat down and turned his chair slightly so that he could see the pool and the swimmers. He looked thoughtful and handsome with his face partly in profile. She looked away, feeling apprehensive suddenly. "What was it you wanted to discuss?"

"I had a lab test carried out in Samoa. There was still a marked depression of Jane's W.B.C., so the prednisone was still working. This is a better remission than I expected. But her tolerance to massive prednisone dosage is gone."

"Mercaptopurine?"

"We don't know until we start what effect, if any, it will have. Her present remission can't last much longer. I doubt she will be active when we reach Fiji. Her condition at Auckland will depend on her reaction to the change in therapy. If she survives to reach Auckland."

Lindy stared at him. "She must!"

So he knew! She was frightened suddenly, and it showed in her eyes. She looked away quickly.

"It would be unfortunate if her husband

joined the ship too late, I agree. Reinhart must have gone to some trouble to arrange what he believes to be a reconciliation between them. It's unfortunate, too, that he happens to be a journalist and not a doctor, and doesn't understand Jane's possible reaction."

"Is it wrong to want to bring two people who love each other together when one has a terminal disease and needs the other?"

"I don't doubt his motives. Or yours, if you prompted him in any way. Now that Carmody is coming, I can tell you that it's something I've wanted myself. However, there are risks—emotional disturbance, shock—and I didn't have the courage to take them. You know why, don't you? Reinhart told you what happened to me in the East."

She stared at him blankly. "Peter, I. . . . !"

"He told you on the beach near Papeete that day. I killed a girl. . . ."

"No, *you didn't*! That wasn't the way he put it at all! Shane told me he knew that you were right. He felt that he had to tell me about it because I'd heard what he called you. He wanted me to know what really happened."

"Reinhart said that?"

"Yes, he did! He's quick tempered, and you'd annoyed him. He was sorry as soon as he'd said it. But all the time he believed you were in the right. Why do you think his newspaper backed you?"

He was staring at her, his face pale beneath the tan as he remembered. "The press was like the board, they were after my hide. But there was one newspaper. . . ."

"His. And if he hadn't believed in you and stepped in to back you up, what do *you* think would have happened?"

"They would have taken away my license. . . ." he said slowly. "So it was Shane Reinhart? I was wrong about him."

"Of course you were wrong about him. He pretends to be tough and cynical, but he isn't really. And that day at the beach, he wouldn't have harmed me. He's gentle. . . ." She broke off, breathing hard, then stood up. "You're wrong about so many things you make me furious!"

"You're in love with him," he said in an odd, hushed voice. But she did not answer. She was walking quickly back across the terrace, her eyes full of angry tears.


Lindy hardly noticed when the ship berthed in Suva. The martial music of a band brought her wearily on deck to see fuzzy-haired Fijian soldiers in scarlet tunics and dazzling white kilt-like sulus with scalloped hems.

A tropical city spread around the shores of a blue bay and climbed partway up the mountain behind it. Fijian traffic police, in white sulus like the soldiers, controlled the bustling waterfront traffic.

As she stared down from the boat deck someone came up behind her and put his hand on hers.

"Miss Livingstone, I presume?"

"Is it as bad as that, Shane," she laughed, looking up at him.

"Worse. Do you realize you've only had one date with me in the past three days. I'm beginning to wonder what you do in the hospital all the time. There are three of you, and both the other girls take time out for relaxation."

She smiled. "There's always something to do."

"With one bed occupied, a couple of diabetics, and the Calvert kid?" he asked, exasperated.

"You're way off, Shane. We have thirty-four patients on the books," she explained. "They come and go."

"Make the others share more of the load,

then. I like to see you around sometimes." He grew serious. "It's Jane, isn't it?"

She nodded. "Auckland next stop, Shane. And she isn't responding so well. She has to improve before he joins the ship."

He frowned. "Yes, I know. I've been thinking about that too. That's why I haven't worried you before. It's just got to work, hasn't it? It would be terrible if she missed him."

She looked at him quickly, startled. "Why did you say that?"

"There's a cyclone moving across the Coral Sea. They've christened it Dora, and it's running wild. Gale force winds and heavy rain over the New Zealand coast. The airports could close."

It was not the same reason that had come to her own mind. But this was a new hazard, one that she hadn't thought about.

"What would happen if the New Zealand airports closed?"

He shrugged. "They'd divert the aircraft here. To Nandi Airport. They'd be grounded here until the weather cleared."

"Oh, no!" she said in dismay.

He patted her hand reassuringly. "Cheer up. It hasn't happened yet. The weather could clear. Lindy, you're all tensed up. Come ashore with me. This is an interesting place, and would be a new experience for you. Please?"

She sighed and nodded. "Tomorrow?"

"All day? It will take me that long to unwind you."

"Well . . . okay!" she smiled.

Going ashore with Shane she felt eager and renewed again. Suva was full of interesting little shops selling bright Indian cloth. The stores were full of duty-free bargains.

The people fascinated her. Indian women walked gracefully past in figure-hugging saris. Indian men in baggy shorts, Sikhs in white turbans, Fijians, Chinese, British colonials in spotless whites, all rubbed shoulders nonchalantly, unaware of any racial difference.

Shane rented a car and drove her along a winding road that reminded her of Tahiti. But when the car stopped at a beach the coral beds were far out, and although the coral was beautiful, viewed through a glass-bottomed boat it wasn't the same.

When they returned to the ship she went directly to the hospital. Sue Bainbridge smiled at her as she entered.

"Have fun ashore?" she asked, and added

quickly. "Peter just left. You can smile again, honey! He says Jane Carmody is showing signs of responding. He said if you happened to look in tonight to tell you he thinks she could be out of bed when we reach Auckland."

"Thank God!" she whispered. "Sue, I *am* glad. . . ."

She did not go ashore in Suva again. Instead she watched Jane Carmody's remission begin, slower this time as Peter Raymond predicted. And as the *Nirvana* sailed toward New Zealand the Pacific began to change slowly too. It became a gray, sullen sea with scudding clouds, and there was a rush for sea-sickness pills and sedatives.

Lindy watched the weather anxiously, and then as they approached Waitemata Harbor and the city of Auckland, miraculously the sky began to clear, the wind to drop.

She was on duty when Bernard Carmody came aboard. Peter Raymond had arranged to have him brought directly to his cabin.

When they came in together, walking slowly, she stood up anxiously. He was a tall, distinguished man with graying hair and steady brown eyes that tried to smile at her as he came into the hospital. His face still held the grayish pallor of shock, and she knew Peter had told him the news.

Peter Raymond said quietly, "Mr. Carmody, this is the nurse I told you about—Miss Madison."

He took her hand. "I don't know how to thank you for what you have done for my wife. I'm lucky she was in such good hands."

She had dreaded this part of it. She realized now that the real strain was on Peter Raymond, and she looked at him sympathetically.

"Sit down, Mr. Carmody," he said quietly. "Seeing you is going to be a shock for your wife. She has to be . . . prepared for it."

"Yes, I know."

"I'll call you in when she's ready. You can take it from there. Miss Madison and I will be here if you should need us."

Carmody nodded and sat down as the door closed behind Peter Raymond.

"God," he muttered. "If I'd only known. . . !" He looked up at her and Lindy saw tears in his eyes. "Is she very much . . . changed?"

She managed to smile. "She's a wonderful woman, Mr. Carmody. She's a little thinner and weaker, but still lovely. She's as bright as ever, and very courageous."

"She was always those things, Miss Madison." He moved uneasily, trying not to look at the closed door. He said gruffly, "Of course, she may not want to see me."

She hesitated. "Mr. Carmody, I've talked quite a lot to your wife. She will see you when she knows you're here. I think it's something that she's wanted for a long time."

His eyes pleaded with her. "You really think so?"

"I know," she said firmly. "She's very much in love with you. And she needs you."

The door was opening. Holding it, Peter Raymond said quietly, "Will you come in, please?"

Bernard Carmody got up unsteadily. He straightened and went in, walking more briskly as he passed Peter Raymond.

She heard Peter Raymond say cheerfully, "Here's your visitor, Mrs. Carmody."

Beyond him she could see into the other room through the open door. Jane Carmody was sitting up expectantly.

If either spoke, she did not hear. Bernard Carmody was on his knees beside the bed suddenly, and his arms were around his wife.

She became aware that she was crying and

that Peter Raymond was closing the door softly. He looked at her and smiled.

"You were right. They're still in love. So maybe it will work out. . . ."

## CHAPTER NINE

The table steward smiled apologetically as he lurched against her chair. "Sorry, Miss Madison."

Lindy smiled at him. Most of the tables were empty, and crossing the dining room had became a precarious business. Plates slid about, and drinking coffee had become an unnerving experience. Shane Reinhart had moved to her table, with Merle Burton and Peter Raymond joining them.

When the wind began to howl and the seas to rise a day's sail from the New Zealand coast, Lindy suddenly became as busy as she had been in the casualty department of a city hospital.

She had never seen people who looked so stricken as the seasick, and there were dozens of them despite the pills the nurses handed out.

Cyclone Dora had started off for Japan from the Coral Sea, leaving a trail of destruction. Then as the *Nirvana* left port it had changed course and was now flattening plantations and houses in the New Hebrides and moving closer to the northern reaches of the Tasman Sea.

But at least she was not seasick like Beth, who had disappeared into her cabin in the first hour of the storm and was still there.

Shane nudged her and said in a low voice, "Here come the lovebirds!" Lindy looked up and saw Bernard and Jane Carmody crossing toward them. Her husband was helping her across the tilting floor, and the way she looked up at him and smiled made Lindy want to cry.

Jane was being nursed in her own cabin now, and there was no longer any problem of keeping her under observation. Bernard was there.

"Hi!" said Shane, grabbing at his plate as it began to slide away from him. "Can't someone make this tub stand still? Jane, you'd better sit down with us. It's safer."

Jane Carmody smiled at her husband affectionately. "Bernard is taking me back to the cabin, Shane. He thinks I'm safer there. I keep telling him I'm fine, but he won't believe me."

"Dr. Raymond said she must rest as much as possible," Bernard said apologetically. He looked at Peter Raymond. "Right, Doctor?"

"This is the first time I've had anyone in authority who could persuade her to do that. I'll call in at ten thirty if I can make it. Or send Miss Madison."

"Thanks, we'll be waiting for you."

Bob Martin had just come in and was sitting down. Jane Carmody said, "What can we expect today, Bob?"

Martin grinned. "Plenty of fun and games. Wind between nine and ten on the Beaufort scale. Heavy seas. Rain squalls most of the day. Cheer up, though, it's starting to clear off the Australian coast, and that's where we're going."

As the Carmodys left, Lindy asked, "What is nine and ten on the Beaufort scale, Mr. Martin?"

"Gale force winds of between fifty and sixty miles an hour. Unpleasant, but not dangerous to a ship this size. This is just a zephyr compared to Dora."

Lindy looked at Shane. "Shane, I'll have to go. Beth's seasick, and that only leaves Sue and me."

He stood up. "I'll help you get to the hospital. Walking isn't very easy."

With his hand on her arm it wasn't so difficult. Every now and then as they crossed the dining room she felt the ship was falling away beneath her, and then it would disconcertingly rise again.

It was better once she reached the hospital near the center of the ship. As Shane left and she went to work, she found her body adjusting to the right balance again. She soon forgot her nervousness in the rush of work from sick and frightened passengers.

The morning passed quickly and at lunchtime she could find time for only a hasty word with Shane—time enough to accept a date in the Tahitian Club whenever she might be lucky enough to get there.

Although Cyclone Dora was still whirling eastward, the weather over the Tasman was getting worse. By midafternoon there was a standing order forbidding passengers to use the decks, and three people in the Tahitian Club had contrived to fall in a tangled heap, resulting in two sprained ankles and a broken finger.

Lindy was glad that Shane had appeared and was waiting for her when the day ended. With his help she made the Tahitian Club, where he steered her to a corner table.

"The stewards have got it easy tonight," he grinned. "The cocktails are all shaking themselves. Sit in the corner, and that way nobody will finish up in our laps. They should put safety belts on those barstools in weather like this."

"Who wants a barstool?" she muttered. She gasped and looked up at the lights in sudden fright as the room vibrated and the lights flickered. "What was that?" she asked nervously.

"That was a really big one. The screws cleared the water there for a moment," Shane explained.

Then the loudspeakers came to life suddenly as she sipped her drink.

"Attention please. Will passengers in cabins two-eight-zero to two-nine-four on upper deck please leave immediately and proceed to the nearest public room. Repeat. All passengers in upper deck cabins two-eight-zero to two-nine-four proceed immediately to the children's playroom. There is no need for alarm. An electrical failure has caused a blackout, and until the trouble is rectified it is necessary for those passengers to leave their cabins."

"Are you sure that's all it is?" Lindy asked nervously. "Shane, look!"

Bob Martin was walking in quickly. He stopped and spoke to Peter Raymond in a low voice. Peter nodded and began to get up. Martin then crossed the room to the officers at the other table and they all left together.

"Shane," she murmured, "something's wrong! They didn't even finish their drinks."

"I noticed," he said, frowning. "Look, honey, it's probably nothing to worry about. Just a short in the wiring someplace."

"I think I should go back to the hospital. Someone could be hurt."

He shook his head. "Let's not panic, Lindy. I'll go down and find out what it's all about. You stay here."

"I'll come with you!" She stood up, but he shook his head. He had turned and was striding away toward the elevator. She sat down again slowly, her apprehension growing steadily.

The steward came over. "Would you like another drink, Miss Madison?"

"No, thank you." She made up her mind suddenly. "Joe, I'm going too! When Mr. Reinhart comes back, will you tell him I've gone to the hospital?"

"Sure, Miss."

The elevator was stationary at the main-deck level, the arrow pointing upward. She hesitated, then started down the stairs. Turning at the landing she heard a babble of voices. Officers were shepherding passengers up the stairs, some still obviously seasick, a few with wraps around them.

"Let me through, please," she said as they blocked her way.

One of the officers called, "Nobody is allowed down there, Miss. You must go back."

"It's me, Miss Madison! What's happening?"

He recognized her and beckoned. "Sorry! Let the nurse through, please! There's a small fire in a couple of cabins," he told her. "We've isolated it, and we'll have it under control in a few minutes. Keep moving there! Keep moving. . . !"

"Fire?" she thought in horror. "Oh, God! No! Not a fire in weather like this. . . ."

She remembered that Shane was down there and began forcing her way down, searching frantically for him. She reached the deck level, panting and bruised. She began to smell smoke coming from the passage on the right of the elevator.

The lights near the elevator had a blue, hazy look, and someone was coming, followed by a steward carrying a stretcher. She recognized the tall figure in uniform.

"Peter!"

Peter Raymond turned quickly. "Lindy! What are you doing here?"

"I thought I might be needed. Have you seen Shane?"

"No. I just got here. There's someone

trapped in there. I might need help. Come on, let's find out what's happening."

Crewmen running out hose let them pass. There was a lot of smoke filling the passage, and through it they saw a disconcerting glow.

"There you are, Doctor!" the chief officer said. "There's a man in one of the burning cabins. Two-nine-zero. Come on there! Get the water flowing! Mr. Clarke, I thought you said all the passengers in the block were accounted for?"

"They are, sir. Miss Moore has cabin two-nine-zero, where the fire started. She fainted and they've taken her to the hospital. But someone said they saw a man go into the cabin."

"It was one of the passengers, sir," a steward said. "Asked me which cabin was burning. I told him two-nine-zero, and said Miss Moore was safe. But he said, where's the child? Then he pushed past me and went in! I saw him!"

"Oh, no!" Lindy cried, and felt Peter Raymond's hand grip her arm.

"What is it, Lindy?"

"That girl! Francine Moore! Shane said she's been bringing the Calvert child down here. Shane must think Jan Calvert is still in there."

"Stay here!" Peter Raymond was gone suddenly, vanishing into the smoke.

"Dr. Raymond, come back!" a voice shouted.

"Stand clear of the extinguishers!" a voice roared. Then, "Doctor, hold it! He's coming out, carrying someone! Play that hose on him, you men! Splash it downward! Quick, he's all right!"

Lindy stood there trembling, horrified and close to fainting. Steam mingled with the smoke now, and an angry hissing sound drowned the voices. Movement started, coming back slowly toward where she stood. An officer was carrying the child, wrapped in a wet blanket. Peter Raymond had his arm around a man with charred clothes dripping water.

"Who is it?" the chief officer demanded.

"It's one of the passengers, sir," the man carrying the child said. "Mr. Reinhart."

"And the child?"

"The Calvert child."

"Get Mr. Reinhart to the hospital," the chief officer ordered.

Peter Raymond said, "Prentice, bring that stretcher. Miss Madison!"

As she and Prentice came out of the smoke and steam, Shane was protesting in a choked, hoarse voice that he didn't need any goddamn stretcher. But Peter made him lie on it anyway, and Prentice covered him with a blanket. Peter Raymond seemed to have lost his coat somewhere, and his shirt was charred and wet. Then she saw Shane's burned hands and face and didn't see anything else. . . .

His eyelids were scorched and he was having difficulty in seeing her, but he knew she was there.

"Going to be . . . all right," he muttered. "That little fool, Francine!"

She felt Peter Raymond's hand on her shoulder. "Lindy, I think you'd better go ahead and get ready for us. You know what to do for third degree burns. There are also two crewmen with burned hands. Sue will have to look after them. Have someone get Beth on her feet. We'll need her too."

She obeyed instinctively. Beth, she knew, would be useless tonight. She thought suddenly of Merle Burton. Mrs. Burton had been a nurse. . . .

One of the longest nights of her life was about to begin.

They had Shane Reinhart on the table and were cutting away the charred clothes when the loudspeakers outside boomed, and they stopped to listen.

"Attention! This is Captain Taylor. The fire in the cabins on the upper deck has been brought completely under control. We anticipate no further danger. All cabins with the exception of two-nine-zero and two-nine-two will be ready for use by noon. I would like to thank all concerned for the way they behaved during the emergency. Thank you everyone, and good night."

"And that's that," Merle Burton said.

She was working smoothly with them, a far better nurse than Beth Kent could ever be, as good a nurse as Lindy, Peter Raymond thought as the last shreds of Shane's clothing were cut away.

He bent, frowning as he examined the extent of the burns. Fifteen percent of the body at least. Mostly third degree. The child could have died in that holocaust. She had been exposed to the heat from the moment the croup lamp fell from the table and set the drapes alight beside the bed. Yet she had only superficial burns, and no noticeable lung damage from smoke.

But Reinhart. . . ?

Peter Raymond began the debridement and cleansing of deeply burned tissues. The task he was attempting began to absorb him. He was going to need a cutdown and drip as soon as he finished the cleansing. Penicillin IV. Plasma to counteract the loss of fluids.

And he must consider the cosmetic angle as he worked. Reinhart wasn't handsome now, with raw flesh on his face, but he would be again. There were plastic surgeons in Sydney as good as any in the world.

So cut carefully, he thought. Don't damage any viable tissues. Keep thinking how the wounds will best heal and cover. Visualize the skin grafts.

He became aware at last that his task was ended. The wounds were surgically clean, the plasma and antibiotic feeding into the patient's veins already fighting infection and shock. He looked at the two women and saw how exhausted they were.

Outside a gray dawn would be coming to the unruly sea. He said gruffly, "That's all we can do for him now. You'd better call it a day. He's going to be all right. He'll have plastic surgery in Sydney, but he'll hold till then. They'll want to wait until he's strong enough to take it and the shock has passed. I'll arrange that when we get there. Merle, will you call Sue Bainbridge. I want her in here with him."

He remembered the two crewmen again. He would have to check what Sue had done. They too would need cleansing surgery.

Lindy said quietly, "I want to stay with him, Peter."

"I'll give you one hour. Then Sue comes in. He won't know you're here until halfway through the morning. Then you can come back." He looked at Merle Burton. "Merle, you were great!"

Merle said as they walked out together, "I'd like to have ten minutes alone with that Moore girl. . . ."

Lindy drew up a chair and sat down wearily and looked at the man in the bed. There was not much to see the way his face and hands were covered with dressings.

"It isn't going to happen again," she thought. "It can't. Peter won't let it happen. . . ."

## CHAPTER TEN

The outside of the hospital in Sydney was gray and old and unimpressive, but the room where Shane Reinhart lay in bed was bright, with wide windows that showed him a green park and a concrete highway. Beyond, trees and gardens sloped gently down to the blue water of a fine harbor, and old British colonial houses alternated with the concrete and glass of tall apartment buildings that clothed the opposite shore.

Lindy was sitting on the chair beside Shane's bed, staring out the window thoughtfully. He studied her profile silently for a while before he said, "Peter Raymond was here this morning."

She looked back at him and smiled. "Yes, he told me."

"The *Nirvana* will be sailing soon. The repairs are almost through. I won't be on it."

Her hand touched his arm and rested there. "I wish you could be."

"A guy can't have everything, Lindy. Peter said the doctor who is going to do my grafts is good. He said there won't be any facial scars. I'm inclined to believe anything Peter says these days, and I'm going to owe that to him. The surgeon here told me Peter had made it easy for him. He said Peter's a fine surgeon."

"He always was," she said. "*You* knew that."

"I guess I did. He's a pretty good guy."

"He said that about you, Shane. And he was right. What you did that night was wonderful."

"Sure! I should get a medal. If I'd stopped to think what I was doing, I'd still be running. But that's me. Rush into things and think about it later."

"I know people who are glad you're like that. The Calverts, Jane and her husband, Peter. . . ."

"But not you. Because I didn't rush anything with you. For once I tried to do everything slow and easy because it seemed to me to be the way you wanted it." His tone had changed. "I'm beginning to regret that. It wasn't like me, and my timing was bad. The ship is sailing, and I'm left behind. Maybe it's too late."

She looked away from him and out the window. "Too late for what, Shane?"

"You know what I mean, Lindy. Could you love a guy looking like this, with only his eyes, mouth, and nose visible? Could you marry a guy who looks like the invisible man on the late-night show?"

She looked back at him, her gray eyes troubled. "Shane, you're the kind of man any girl could love for what you are. Even if you *were* scarred, it wouldn't matter."

He shook his head slightly. "Don't fence with me. I'm not asking *any* girl, I'm asking you."

"Shane, I . . . !" She looked away, confused.

"I'm not very good at this. Probably because I've spent my life so far avoiding it. So there's something I forgot to mention. I love you."

"Shane," she murmured. "I don't know what to say. I'm fond of you, but that isn't love. With Roy it was different. He needed me. And the way I felt in return . . . wasn't a bodily need, it was . . . ideal. I feel differently about you. I think if you'd wanted me in Tahiti, I would have given myself to you. But that wouldn't have been love."

"*Now* she tells me!" he said. "Lindy, I've got

news for you. This other thing you spoke about, that wasn't love either! No, hear me out, please! The guy was sick, he had to be since he died. You haven't told me much about it, and I didn't ask because I didn't want to hurt you. But you're a nurse and you *must* have known. So don't tell me pity didn't come into it. Sympathy. A desire to help and encourage and heal the guy. Because you're you, it couldn't be otherwise."

"It isn't as simple as that. . . !" She was thinking suddenly of Peter Raymond. He had said something like that too.

"No," he said quietly. "It isn't. Because love has to be a little of both. It has to be idealistic, yes. But it has to be physical too. One is no good without the other. You can't love a man with your mind."

"I've hurt you, made you angry. I'm sorry Shane. I can't help the way I feel about these things."

He shook his head. "I'm not angry with you, Lindy. I don't think I could be. I think I've known since Tahiti that you were not in love with me. But neither were you in love with this guy Roy. Maybe you're in love with someone who is a little of each of us. Someone who has physical attraction and idealism too. You know who I mean."

She frowned, remembering. "At Tahiti you were jealous of Peter. You were wrong, Shane. You shouldn't have been."

"Why not? He was in love with you, and a long time before that. Why do you think he came charging down the beach that way?" He eased up against his pillows and sighed. "I'm getting all steamed up! Lindy, if I can't have you I would still like to see you happy. I think you've been in love with Peter Raymond for a long while. That other was just . . . something that intervened. Think about what I said. And don't leave it till it's too late. I don't think Peter will be on the *Nirvana* next year."

She stood on the promenade deck as the S.S. *Nirvana* glided out from the harbor and steamed slowly toward Sydney Heads and the open sea. From his window beyond the harbor shore she knew that Shane would be watching the ship leave.

She was sailing out of Shane's life, and the thought saddened her. But Shane, she knew, would find another girl, would play the field again until he found the right one. He deserved the best, not a girl like herself who didn't know her own mind or what she wanted. A girl who had grown confused and uncertain even about memories she had once treasured.

She became aware that somebody was standing beside her at the rail, and she looked up and smiled at Peter Raymond.

"When will you see Shane again?" he asked quietly. "At the end of the cruise?"

"Maybe not."

Seagulls were circling above the bridge and he stared up at them briefly. "I thought Shane was in love with you," he said almost angrily.

"He thought so too."

"And you with him."

"No," she said. "I was never in love with Shane."

He took out his pipe and began to pack tobacco into the bowl. "Reinhart could make you happy. He's a good man. You can't live forever in the past."

She sighed. "I know it now. Shane taught me that. You tried to tell me too, but I wouldn't listen."

"Lindy I've often thought how much I'd like to be able to put the clock back. But that isn't possible. Too much has happened in between. To both of us."

"I've thought so too," she said slowly. She was thinking of the things Shane Reinhart had said. Shane was wise in his own way. Shane knew people. . . .

"Remember that party?" he said. He smiled. "I wanted another date with you badly, but it didn't seem to work out. I was offered the New York thing, and there were arrangements to make, all sorts of urgent things to be done. Then I meant to see you and say good-bye, but that didn't work out either. Believe it or not, I was very much in love with you at the time. If I'd thought you might have said yes, I would have asked you to marry me and go with me. But that was stupid of course. To you I was just another date."

"No, you weren't. I . . . had an awful crush on you too. I . . . might have said yes."

"God!" he said. "If I had known that. . . ." He broke off. "Lindy, I don't suppose we could start again where we left off? I mean, be friends like we were then. Get to know each other all over again?"

"I. . . ." Her doubts, her memories had all come rushing back. It was as though Shane was prompting her as she looked up at Peter slowly. "I'd like that Peter. I'd like that very much. I think it was what I wanted when I came aboard and you were here. But I didn't know how to tell you, and you had other things on your mind."

"Lindy, I was a fool! I. . . ."

The voice of the intercom cut across his words. "Attention, Dr. Raymond. Dr. Raymond, you are wanted in the captain's office."

"Don't go away," he said anxiously.

"No. And don't you go away, Peter. Not again. . . ."

She watched him stride across the deck and wished Shane could have seen them standing at the rail.

She whispered, "Thank you, Shane! Thank you!"

Other SIGNET Nurse-Doctor Romances
You Will Enjoy

- ☐ **DOCTOR IN SHADOW by Diana Douglas.** A promising young surgeon returning home from a two-year stay in London faces emotional and professional ruin.
(#D3204—50¢)

- ☐ **DR. HOLLAND'S NURSE by Jane Converse.** The story of a beautiful young nurse who is torn between honor and desire—between the man she had promised to marry and the man she loves. (#D3161—50¢)

- ☐ **EMERGENCY NURSE by Jane Converse.** A tense, dramatic novel of a nurse and doctor who fight to save a girl's life, a baby's future . . . and their own shattered love. (#D3125—50¢)

- ☐ **HEARTBREAK NURSE by Jane Converse.** A nurse finds that the man she loves expects her to give her own life for a beautiful nightmare out of his past.
(#D3683—50¢)

- ☐ **A NURSE TO MARRY by Patti Carr.** A young nurse is torn between her strong dedication to medicine and her love for the exciting and handsome young doctor. (#P3841—60¢)

---

**THE NEW AMERICAN LIBRARY, INC., P.O. Box 2310, Grand Central Station, New York, New York 10017**

Please send me the SIGNET BOOKS I have checked above. I am enclosing $_____(check or money order—no currency or C.O.D.'s). Please include the list price plus 10¢ a copy to cover mailing costs. (New York City residents add 6% Sales Tax. Other New York State residents add 3% plus any local sales or use taxes.)

Name_____

Address_____

City_____State_____Zip Code_____

Allow at least 3 weeks for delivery

- ☐ **MARILYN MORGAN, R.N. by Rubie Saunders.** Happy with her work at the city hospital Marilyn Morgan now faces the most serious decision of her career.
 (#P3946—60¢)

- ☐ **ART COLONY NURSE by Jane Converse.** A respectable nurse by day and by night a uninhibited woman who found love and excitement at an art colony, is the double life that Eileen finds herself leading in this novel of romance and intrigue. (#P3927—60¢)

- ☐ **RESORT NURSE by Diana Douglas.** Drugs, hippies, a a wealthy writer and a handsome doctor nearly cause disaster for Nurse Spencer. (#P3894—60¢)

- ☐ **DUTY NURSE by Diana Douglas.** A triangle of tragedy played out by a doctor, patient and nurse.
 (#T3987—75¢)

- ☐ **EXPEDITION NURSE by Jane Converse.** A nurse is one of five people thrown together in the search for an ancient Peruvian temple, an expedition that yields danger, threats . . . and their undiscovered selves.
 (#D3608—50¢)

**THE NEW AMERICAN LIBRARY, INC.,** P.O. Box 2310, Grand Central Station, New York, New York 10017

Please send me the SIGNET BOOKS I have checked above. I am enclosing $_____(check or money order—no currency or C.O.D.'s). Please include the list price plus 10¢ a copy to cover mailing costs. (New York City residents add 6% Sales Tax. Other New York State residents add 3% plus any local sales or use taxes.)

Name_____

Address_____

City_____State_____Zip Code_____
Allow at least 3 weeks for delivery

## SIGNET Gothics You Will Enjoy

- [ ] **THE OUIJA BOARD by Teri Lester.** A tropical vacation becomes a devil's paradise when a young girl's death is predicted by the ouija board. (#P4011—60¢)

- [ ] **SUFFER A WITCH TO DIE by Elizabeth Davis.** A macabre spell plunges a young woman in a nightmare of horror in this novel of reincarnation. (#T4097—75¢)

- [ ] **HARVEST OF TERROR by Adela Gale.** With romantic Majorca as its background this is an exceptionally exciting Gothic tale of suspense. (#P4044—60¢)

- [ ] **HOUSE OF DESTINY by Caroline Farr.** A chilling tale of a beautiful girl's harrowing experience in an old house. (#T4109—75¢)

- [ ] **FALCONLOUGH by Monica Heath.** A Gothic novel of horror ranging in setting from the relic of St. Kevin's church in Glendalough, Ireland to the California coastline and an eerie castle filled with strange dreams, mysterious deaths, and uncanny coincidences. (#D2875—50¢)

---

**THE NEW AMERICAN LIBRARY, INC., P.O. Box 2310, Grand Central Station, New York, New York 10017**

Please send me the SIGNET BOOKS I have checked above. I am enclosing $_____(check or money order—no currency or C.O.D.'s). Please include the list price plus 10¢ a copy to cover mailing costs. (New York City residents add 6% Sales Tax. Other New York State residents add 3% plus any local sales or use taxes.)

Name_____

Address_____

City_____State_____Zip Code_____

Allow at least 3 weeks for delivery

# NOW! FOR THE FIRST TIME EVER!

**Your PERSONAL HOROSCOPE Charted for You Only by World-Famous Astrologer, Katina Theodossiou and the IBM/360 Computer.**

Combining modern technology with over 30 years of astrological experience, Miss Theodossiou presents in-depth horoscopes that would take weeks to prepare and would cost up to $300 if charted by the traditional method. Cast from your own day, year, time, and place of birth, your 25-30 page Time Pattern Report will provide startling infomation about you and only you, for no two reports are ever alike. Projecting into the year ahead, your personal chart covers your character, health, material potentials, romance, and the *select actual dates* that are of special significance to you alone. And there is no risk involved. If you are not completely satisfied with your Time Pattern Report within ten days, your money will be refunded in full. Simply fill out the coupon below. Please allow three weeks for delivery.

---

**THE NEW AMERICAN LIBRARY/DEPT. L.W.**
**1301 Ave. of the Americas, New York, N.Y. 10019**

Enclosed find $20. (Check or Money Order—No Currency or C.O.D.'s) New York City residents add 6% Sales Tax. Other New York State residents add 3% plus any local sales or use taxes.

Please prepare my confidential, in-depth Time Pattern Report, which includes projections for the year ahead. I understand that if I am not completely satisfied with my Time Pattern Report within ten days, my money will be refunded in full.

| DATE OF BIRTH | PLACE OF BIRTH | TIME OF BIRTH |
|---|---|---|
| Month_____ | City_____ | _____A.M. |
| Day_____ | State_____ | _____P.M. |
| Year_____ | Country_____ | _____Don't Know |
| | Mr. ☐      Mrs. ☐      Miss ☐ | |

Name_____

Address_____

City_____ State_____ Zip_____